Anne Berest is a Parisian author and journalist. She also writes for television, cinema and theatre. She was working on her third novel when Françoise Sagan's son, Denis Westhoff, asked her to write a book to mark the sixtieth anniversary of the publication of *Bonjour Tristesse*.

Heather Lloyd was previously Senior Lecturer in French at the University of Glasgow, and has published work on Françoise Sagan. She is the most recent translator of *Bonjour Tristesse* for Penguin.

Sagan, Paris 1954

GALLIC

Sagan, Paris 1954

Anne Berest

Translated from the French by Heather Lloyd

Gallic Books
London

A Gallic Book

First published in France as *Sagan 1954* by Éditions Stock, 2014
Copyright © Éditions Stock, 2014

English translation copyright © Gallic Books 2015
First published in Great Britain in 2015 by Gallic Books, 59 Ebury Street, London,
SW1W 0NZ

Photographic Credits:
p18. © Thomas D. McAvoy/Getty Images
p76. © Jacques Rouchon/Roger-Viollet
p96. © All rights reserved
p111. © Sabine Weiss/Gamma Rapho
p120. © Thomas D. McAvoy/Getty Images

A CIP record for this book is available from the British Library
ISBN 978-1-908313-89-8

Typeset in Fournier MT by Gallic Books
Printed and bound by CPI Group (UK) Ltd, Croydon, CR0 4YY

2 4 6 8 10 9 7 5 3

To my parents
To Martine Saada

Without Sagan, life would be deadly boring.
Bernard Frank

I see a man of sixty-five leaving the New Year's Eve party that has been organised in his honour, like someone walking out of their bedroom leaving the bed unmade. In any case, wherever he is going, the party's over. Once, he made the heart of Paris beat faster, but today there is no one left for him to dance with: those he can truly converse with are dead – or have not yet been born.

I imagine a car in Rue de Montpensier dropping him off in the half-light of a day that is still hovering between the old year and the new. A young couple are just passing the impressive entrance to his home, whispering to each other.

The man watches the two figures as they scuttle through the cold of that early morning. He notices the way they pull each other along by the arm, like two crabs heading in the direction of the Seine. The young boy is not bad-looking, with his Joan of Arc haircut – like a page boy who has been lifted straight out of an illuminated manuscript.

It seems to me that these two characters, shining through the dawn, pass Cocteau without recognising him. I can hear the two teenagers break into ripples of laughter as they run off towards the Palais-Royal.

If you look more closely and if you listen to their high-pitched peals of mirth, you realise that they are both girls. One is called Françoise and the other Florence. Whenever they race each other through the streets of Paris, neither one wins. In the end Françoise always holds out her hand to Florence and draws her along at her own swift pace.

*

Over the coming months I am going to be writing a book about Françoise Sagan and it is with that scene, featuring Cocteau and the daybreak, that I would like to begin it.

My book is to be a journal of the year 1954, telling the story of the few months leading up to publication of *Bonjour Tristesse*.

A few months is not a very long time.

But I am going through one of the most painful periods of my life. Since the summer, I have been separated from the father of my daughter. I am weighed down by misery and I feel like a suitcase without a handle.

I am going to put an end to my grief through work. Night and day I am going to think about Sagan; day and night she will be my companion.

This will give me the best excuse for not seeing anyone: I have to read all the biographies, all the novels and all the interviews. Sagan gives me the courage to do this; she is the best possible source of comfort.

In my notebook with its brown paper cover I jot down phrases that I've gleaned here and there. I collect them, as I would the wise counsels of an older friend, a woman who has seen it all and who knows, therefore, that there is no advice to be given, that experience cannot be passed on and that the only thing we are able to bequeath to others is the testimony of our own existence, that is to say, the mere fact of it, which is the proof that people can come through every sort of situation and that happiness can sometimes return.

I make myself at home with her, just as I make myself at home in the various flats that people lend me these days. I borrow my friend Catherine's shoes. I spray myself with Esther's perfume, in her bathroom. I slip into the mindset of Françoise Sagan as if I were slipping on a pair of silk stockings – I inhabit her life in order to forget my own.

Here she is again with her friend Florence Malraux on the Pont des Arts, just as the new year makes its appearance in the sky above Paris between the Institut de France and the Eiffel Tower.

Ahead of them, the grimy façades of the Parisian buildings look like a huge accordion spilling out along the banks of the Seine. A sense of peace reigns, a thin film of frost covers the preceding years, like those white dust sheets that you throw over the furniture in country houses before you leave.

Thus each new year Paris draws away from the Occupation, transforming events into memories. And in the end, memories are always forgotten.

Florence and Françoise are children of wartime; in other words, strange creatures who began life at the end: they know the real God is Chance. And they know everything can go wrong. With that as your starting point, you've got to make the best of what you have.

They had been in the same class in the Cours Hattemer, a lycée in Rue de Londres, in the district round the Gare Saint-Lazare. It was a private school for children who were 'special cases'.

Owing to a long illness, Florence had had to give up normal state school for a while.

As for Françoise, she had been expelled from every conceivable type of establishment, first from a convent school (le Couvent des Oiseaux) for her 'failure to be deeply spiritual', then from the Louise-de-Bettignies School for having 'hanged a bust of Molière with a piece of string'[1] – though would Molière not have appreciated being hanged in the form of this dreary, scholastic representation?

It was during this period that, as a little girl on her way to morning mass, she would pass the revellers in their dinner jackets, clutching champagne bottles, issuing from the nightclubs on Rue de Ponthieu.[2] She was a child who believed adults had much more fun than children.

(I discover that a convent called 'the Convent of the Birds' really did exist. I used to believe that it was something made up by my mother who, when I was small, used to say about any little girl whom she thought rather silly, 'She comes from the Convent of the Little Birds.')

Françoise had been expelled from several religious establishments, but she did have to pass her *baccalauréat*. Fortunately, in 1885, a Mademoiselle Rose Hattemer had invented a method of learning that stimulated the intelligence rather than the memory. It was thanks to Rose that the two teenage girls met in the little playground of the experimental school.

Françoise was impressed by Florence, for Florence had been in the Resistance with her mother. And Florence was Jewish. (Yet France was not too keen on Jews after the war – they brought back bad memories.)

Florence was fascinated by Françoise because she asked questions that nobody asked. And because her mind worked in unexpected ways. And because she was never mawkish, as girls can be.

The two teenagers were going to become the very best of friends.

They shared a love of literature and they both subscribed to the same principle, namely, that you should treat great matters as if they were of little account and small matters as if they were great ones.

It was something that Françoise had come to understand as a result of the carefree life she had led and that Florence had come to understand as a result of her sombre life.

What they didn't know was that they were going to spend the next fifty years of their lives hand in hand and that it was all going to go by in a flash.

Françoise had read Proust, and Florence, Dostoyevsky.[3] Between them they had the century wrapped up and they swopped books as others swopped taffeta frocks.

But on that first of January 1954, as day breaks over the Pont des Arts, they still barely know each other.

'We must make a vow,' says Françoise.

'Fine,' replies Florence.

And the vow the two girls make is one and the same: they vow that Françoise will find a publisher.

Meanwhile, in Rue de Montpensier, Cocteau, who is ill, falls asleep, as he does every night, thinking of the young man he has loved so much. He is thinking of Radiguet. He thinks of him every second of every hour. Radiguet goes on living in him. And goes on dying too.

For the second scene in this book, I would like to describe Françoise waking up in her childhood bedroom at her parents' home in the elegant Monceau Plain district, at 167 Boulevard Malesherbes.

There, in a vast apartment from the Haussmann era, Pierre and Marie Quoirez, originally from the provinces, have installed their three children. As members of the bourgeoisie, they 'both loved partying and had a liking for Bugattis. They drove round the roads at breakneck speed. My parents were youthful and up-to-the-minute.'[4]

Marie, the mother, is perfect. She is like a brown butterfly with blue wings and always impeccably turned out. She loves to laugh, loves going out, loves to make the most of everything the capital has to offer. Much later, Françoise will say of her that she did not live in the real world, that she was always somewhere else as she rummaged among her hats. But, for the moment, Françoise does not pay much attention to her mother. She has eyes only for her father, her ideal – Pierre. It was for him and by his side that she wrote her manuscript the previous summer, in just six weeks.

Françoise, of course, went to bed late the night before. She had been living it up with her brother Jacques. They had drunk whisky because, with whisky, you sink into a respectable melancholy that does not involve self-loathing – but, even so, this morning her eyelids seem full of grit.

Since daybreak, several people have gone into Françoise's room. The first had been Julia Lafon, the girl from the plains of Cajarc, the limestone plateaux in the Lot. She is the family's housekeeper and she comes in to gather up some blouses from Weill's ready-to-wear collection. Next comes Marie Quoirez to encourage her younger daughter to get up at a suitable hour for a young lady of her age. But, oh well … she's got the rest of her life to get up early.

Pierre, who is an engineer and the technical director of a factory, merely opens the door to look at his big girl sleeping. He remembers stroking her head when she sat on his lap in the Jaguar as a tiny child, her little hands on the wheel.

A yellow pillow lies on the ground, like a block of fresh butter. It's the biggest pillow in the house and Françoise makes sure she has it so that she can read late into the night, comfortably propped up against the wall. The bedside table has a glass top, strewn with magazines and piles of books.

At the foot of the bed, on a fringed rug, an enormous record player is positioned at just the right distance so that Françoise only has to stretch out her arm, without getting out of bed, to turn her records over. On it I picture the Billie Holiday sleeve where you see that wonderful face, with a large flower behind the ear and pearls round her neck, just like Frida Kahlo.

The teenage girl, asleep on this morning of 4 January 1954, whose parents still call her by the pet name of 'Kiki', is far from imagining that in the not too distant future Lady Day will sing for her, in her presence, and will hug her and talk to her as a friend.

In order to put the finishing touches to this tableau – this imaginary representation of Françoise waking up – I have to decide what books will be lying on the bedside table.

Because this is the room of a girl who has set her sights on becoming a writer, I choose *A Room of One's Own* by Virginia Woolf.

I search for the book on my shelves in order to reread certain passages that I would like to quote here.

I study Woolf's words, wondering what Françoise Sagan would have made of them. It's like rediscovering a book you have just given as a present: putting yourself in your loved one's shoes, you wonder what their feelings will be when they read it.

Yes, it's clear that Françoise Sagan loved this book. I have to select two or three sentences from it, although I would like to include them all.

'Why did men drink wine and women water?'

'Of the two – the vote and the money – the money, I own, seemed infinitely the more important.'

'Intellectual freedom depends upon material things' or, again, 'A woman must have money and a room of her own if she is to write fiction.'[5]

The pages of *A Room of One's Own* bring a lump to my throat because I am reminded that when last I read the book I had dreams of becoming a writer and I wondered if one day I would have the necessary strength and courage.

Then my eyes light upon the very first page:

A Room of One's Own

Virginia Woolf

Translated by Clara Malraux

Reading these words, I feel the veins in my neck throb, just as they do when you find something by chance that you hadn't been looking for: a hidden love letter not intended for you; a 500-euro note just when you are short of money; or the offer of a trip when you want to get away from someone.

Clara had translated Virginia Woolf. That is, Clara Malraux, the mother of Sagan's best friend.

So I was fully justified, justified at least in placing that book on Françoise's bedside table. And why not even a copy with a dedication from the translator? 'To Françoise, who will one day be a writer.' For that is what her daughter had told her a few weeks previously, having just read her friend's manuscript at a single sitting: 'Françoise is a writer.'

Now that I have set the scene, with the books, the music and the blouses, I can wake Françoise up. I can get her to rub her eyes like a child, as she does in a photograph taken in Saint-Tropez in which she is wearing a checked nightdress. Then, in the corridors of her parents' apartment, she goes in search of her brother, who is her best friend as far as boys are concerned. Jacques Quoirez is twenty-seven. He has gone off to London to 'get experience' in a business there but he comes back to Paris for the end-of-year festivities. I am struck by the photographs of him that I have found in trawling through archives on the internet. He looks nothing like Françoise – you wouldn't think they came from the same family.

Jacques has read his little sister's manuscript.

Jacques has been impressed by what he has read.

Yet he is not a man to set aside his usual cynical attitude. With his stripy blazers, his threadbare Charvet shirts and his hide moccasins, he is the darling of the circles he moves in. He is blithe and devil-may-care and he possesses what is known as charm, which, in a man of leisure, is a terrible defect.

Not wishing either to flatter her or to fill her with false hope, Jacques has told her that the book she has written is a nice little composition,[6] not at all bad for a first novel. He agrees to help his little sister parcel up the manuscripts, while at the same time giving her a warning: you have to be patient, and very patient at that, if you want to get yourself published. He has friends, some decidedly more gifted than she is and others with better contacts in the publishing world, who are still waiting for replies. Françoise, he muses, will soon discover that life isn't as cushy everywhere as it is in Boulevard Malesherbes. Little

Kiki has been so spoilt and pampered by their parents, Pierre and Marie, that one day she is going to have to be surprised by the real world. But the later the better, he thinks, for at the end of the day he loves his kid sister more than he loves any other woman.

All the same, Jacques has been impressed by 'Franquette'. No one really believed that she would write that mysterious book of hers so quickly. In places he has recognised literary influences: the 'warm, pink' shell like the ham in Rimbaud's 'At the Green Inn'; the words of Cécile, with their echoes of Musset's character Perdican; the quotations from Oscar Wilde and the influence of Choderlos de Laclos. But he has no wish to discourage her; there is nothing more tiresome than critics. We shall see – after all, this is a child who has always got what she wanted, from no matter who.

After much debate, they settle on three publishers, Gallimard, Plon and Julliard. They put the typed manuscripts in big yellow folders and Françoise asks her brother if he will write her address on them. She feels sure that confident masculine handwriting will put the publishers' readers in a positive frame of mind.

Françoise Quoirez,
167 Boulevard Malesherbes.

When he has written the addresses, Jacques has a thought.

Françoise really must put her date of birth on the manuscripts. His hope is that the idea of a little eighteen-year-old will touch the hearts of the readers and that when they return the manuscripts they will perhaps be less nasty in their accompanying letters.

'What if we added the phone number too?' suggests Françoise.

'What for?' asks Jacques.

'In case they want to take me on immediately! In case they really, really like the book!'

'No, Françoise, no. That would look silly. Publishers don't phone you. They send a letter.'

But Françoise is insistent. She agrees to include her date of birth as long as they add the phone number. So, on all three copies, Jacques writes:

Françoise Quoirez,
167 Boulevard Malesherbes.
Carnot 59-61. Date of birth: 21 June 1935.

He suddenly feels very afraid for his little sister.

'Whatever happens, if this one doesn't get published, you will write another, won't you?'

'Yes, of course. It won't be the end of the world.'

'Not even a little bit, OK?'

'I don't write in order to get published, you know. I write because, first and foremost, it's something I enjoy doing.'

'That's just as well.'[7]

Smiling, and as a parting shot before closing the door behind her, Françoise calls out to her brother, 'But I shall get published!'

At that very moment, on that fourth of January 1954, a boy of the same age – eighteen, to be precise – is recording two songs. It costs him four dollars, which he pays for out of his own pocket, and he records them in a small studio specialising in the black soul music of Memphis.

The songs are 'My Happiness' and 'That's When Your Heartaches Begin'.

Both those kids, Françoise Sagan and Elvis Presley, are going to need shoulders broad enough to bear the weight of what they are going to become in a few months' time: two idols pursued by frenzied crowds. But today they have quite simply *done* something, and it all stems from there. You never lose out by just *doing* something; there is a chance you might even win. You have to take on board the risk of winning, and the young do not realise just what the consequences of winning can be.

This is a book I have to write quickly, and it is taking shape and gradually coming into focus.

It is to be neither a biography, nor a journal, nor a novel. Let's just call it a story.

The idea is that it's the story of a girl, a very young girl, writing her first novel.

I will be cataloguing the various stages in the life of a budding author: her excitement, her fearfulness, her sense of anticipation.

My book will be about the progress of another book, from the moment the manuscript is sent off to the point at which it receives a literary prize. My plan is to focus on a few days in one year, the year in which the heroine's life will be turned upside down. With every passing day and week, the anonymous teenager will be on her way to becoming a recognised writer.

If this were a made-up story, I would have to work on the issue of plausibility in order to get the reader to accept that certain incredible things can actually happen. I mean things like a book becoming a huge success while simultaneously causing a monumental scandal; I mean things like a girl who had not yet come of age becoming a social phenomenon and the most famous Frenchwoman of her era.

But that story is true. So my task is to understand and then explain to others how implausible things can suddenly happen in life. I have to be able to show how a book can explode on the scene like a bomb, how it can burst forth like springtime, how it can have an impact like the catastrophe in a Greek tragedy.

'Françoise,' says Jacques, 'are you sure you won't be sad if your novel isn't published?'

'I don't know. We'll see. I like writing.'

'Why do you like writing?' asks Jacques. He can see that his sister does not envisage being met with rejection, still less with indifference.

'To write a novel is to construct a lie. I like telling lies. I have always lied,' she answers laughingly. 'Come on, wish me luck.'[8]

I visualise this girl in the Métro, sitting among other girls. They are all dressed just like their mothers, in long coats down to their ankles, Jacques Fath-style coats in dyed wool, or tweed coats. They wear little silk scarves and have their hair tied back, revealing the few pearls round their necks – there are no pierced ears. They are all dressed severely. It is an era when the transition from childhood to adulthood is a brutal one and there is nothing in between.

Like the others, Françoise is wearing a heavy coat and a red-and-white striped blouse buttoned all the way up. She could be anything from fifteen to thirty.

This is the last stage in her life when Françoise's face is not the face of celebrity. These are the last weeks in the whole of her existence when she is still a girl like other girls, a girl of eighteen. She doesn't know that there's not much of the old life left for her, nor that everything is about to be turned upside down because of what she is carrying, like a cancer, under her arm. Those sheets of paper covered in words, typed up by a friend 'because it's neater like that',[9] are going to change her life for good. But we're not there yet. For the moment, I see her observing people in the reflection of the carriage windows. She feels sorry for a girl who has no ankles and whose calves go straight up and down like broomsticks. It's unfair that some people are not beautiful, she thinks, as she is lulled by the sound of the train.

> Whenever I came across people who weren't physically attractive, I experienced a sort of uneasiness, a sense of lack; the fact that they were resigned to being unattractive struck me as being an unseemly failing on their part. For, after all, what was our aim in life, if not to be pleasing to others?[10]

Françoise had got on at Wagram and had changed at Saint-Lazare, finally to emerge at the exit in Rue du Bac, where the wind blew up under her coat. Turning right into Rue de l'Université, she walks along to number 30, the premises of the publisher Julliard. Her hand is frozen when she pushes open the massive green door, tottering as she does so. She turns round. There is a young man behind her. They barely exchange glances but both guess that they are there for the same reason.

So they approach the desk together and naturally the receptionist addresses the young man.

'Are you here to submit a manuscript?'

'Yes,' he replies timidly.

'Don't bother phoning for a reply. You'll get a letter in a few weeks. If your manuscript is rejected, you can come back here and pick it up.'

'But I don't live near Paris,' he replies.

'In that case, come back with some stamped addressed envelopes. Thank you, and good day to you, Monsieur. Good day, Mademoiselle.'

The young man hurries out in search of a post office and some stamps. Françoise waits politely; she waits patiently and graciously, still facing the woman, who has buried her nose in her work again. 'So sorry, I thought you were with the boy!' exclaims the receptionist when at length she realises her mistake.

'It really doesn't matter,' replies Françoise. 'It really doesn't matter at all. Please don't apologise.'

Now we see Françoise (somewhat lighter, having been relieved of one manuscript) trotting off in the direction of the Librairie Gallimard, the high temple of publishing. This august establishment is only a short walk from Julliard, at number 5 Rue Sébastien-Bottin – the street is called after the man who gave his name to a directory of commerce and industry.

There is no one at reception. She hesitates. Her friend Florence works there but only started a few days ago. It would seem too casual just to wander off down the corridors looking for her.

So Françoise waits, politely, patiently and graciously. A young woman, hurrying past, asks her if she is there to drop off a manuscript. Françoise nods. The young woman reaches forward automatically to take the yellow folder and then declares in a single breath, 'Don't bother phoning for a reply you'll get a letter in a few weeks and if your manuscript is rejected you can come back here and pick it up.'

Françoise's next port of call is Éditions Plon, based in Rue Garancière, a quiet little street that doesn't get too much sun, a pleasant street, its name evoking that of a flower.

I can hear Françoise's footsteps. She is slightly out of breath, wondering, like someone wagering on several numbers in roulette, which number will come up. Which publishing firm will turn her destiny upside down? I see her frail little form, head down, lost in thought when her path crosses that of two men preoccupied by weighty matters.

The two men are of equal height.

The first man is all forehead: it is wide and pale and underneath it is a birdlike face. His beard and large spectacles seem almost to have been stuck on, the features beneath them being so chiselled. He is assistant director at the Musée de l'Homme and, apart from his thesis, he has still only published a single work, with Presses Universitaires de France. Yet, at forty-six, he is no youngster. The second man, the one whose hands dart hither and thither in the air like insects, has his heart set on bringing out *Tristes Tropiques*. This fledgling publisher, much younger than Claude Lévi-Strauss, has black, unruly locks and a generous mouth. Strikingly handsome, he is the first man to have reached the geomagnetic North Pole. Jean Malaurie is launching a new series for Plon, entitled Terre Humaine. He wants it to be the home for a new type of intellectual: author-explorers, men defined solely by the terrain they have covered.

It is this editorial dream that the explorer of Greenland is explaining as he walks along Rue Garancière, with the Senate behind him, while young Françoise passes them coming from the opposite direction, her ankle boots click-clacking on the cobbles.

Françoise goes into an imposing mansion, the Hôtel de Sourdéac, which houses a printing works whose presses are always running at full tilt. But there is also on the premises a publishing firm, one that has made itself particularly receptive to literature and essays, called La Librairie Plon, les petits-fils de Plon & Nourrit.

On entering the courtyard, Françoise is overpowered by the smell of fresh ink, which then catches her by the throat as it mingles with the scent worn by the young woman at reception. Jolie Madame, the latest perfume from Pierre Balmain, is a mixture of violets and leather and has been popular as a gift this last Christmas. Jolie Madame goes through the same rigmarole as her predecessors: Are you submitting a manuscript? You can expect a letter. You'll hear nothing for several weeks, etc.

The die is cast. With her arms now free and swinging by her side, Françoise crosses Place Saint-Sulpice in the cold of that sixth of January. All she is thinking of is dinner that evening, when her big sister Suzanne will be celebrating her thirtieth birthday.

As happens every year, her mother will have bought a huge galette des rois, still warm. And as happens every year, everyone will make sure that Kiki finds the charm hidden in it and gets to wear the crown.

To Françoise, thirty seems a lifetime, too far off to contemplate. She doesn't know that, by the age of thirty, she will have been married and divorced twice, will be a mother, and a writer acclaimed throughout the world, her work adapted for the cinema by Otto Preminger, acted by Jean Seberg and sung by Juliette Gréco; she will be both loved and loathed and, in a terrible accident, she will have come close to death, a place beyond the reach of memory.

Between now and the age of thirty she has so much to experience.

Suddenly I visualise Françoise in the radiance of youth. I am more than thirty now and I feel out of place as – on the run from my own life – I immerse myself in the life of another. I am following in the tracks of a child; I see her cross the square by the side of the church of Saint-Sulpice. She crosses it diagonally, passing close to the fountain and its lions.

Fully preoccupied as she is by the thought of the birthday present she is planning to give her sister, Françoise does not know that she is being watched from behind the façade of the church by the painting by Delacroix.

It is of Jacob wrestling with the Angel.

His raised knee is a sign of his will. His muscular back tells of his resoluteness. And his arm and shoulder bespeak his determination to fight. Every sinew in the magnificent body of the man called Jacob is straining towards victory and, at daybreak, he will gain God's favour because he, a natural man, has wrestled with the supernatural. But his thigh will be for ever marked by the injury he has sustained.

In every combat undertaken, in every task completed, in every victory gained, one must accept that something will be lost.

In every task completed.

In every combat undertaken.

One must accept that something will be lost.

What shall I lose through this book?

I was immersed in the writing of my third novel when, more than ten days ago now, Françoise Sagan's son suggested that I should write a book about his mother. Denis Westhoff is a man of around fifty. Listening to him talk is very pleasant: he speaks rapidly, in a soft, staccato tone, without any hesitation, like the needle of a sewing machine regularly piercing felt.

'We will soon be marking the tenth anniversary of her death, ten years already, and I would like people to remember just what the publication of *Bonjour Tristesse* represented for society back in 1954. That was sixty years ago!'

This proposition is like a sign; it is obvious to me that this is something I *must* do. I drop the book I'm working on for her, for Françoise.

I phone Édouard because I am delighted to tell him the news. But we argue: he says that I feel flattered to set my name alongside Françoise Sagan's and that I should guard against vanity, etc.

I send him an email telling him how hurt I am:

Sometimes your friends attack you with cruel words that hurt. But because they aim true and see in you the things you keep most hidden, they say, 'It's because I care about you that I can see the part of you that you would like to hide. And, seeing that side of you, I still go on caring about you. Perhaps I care about you even more, knowing what I do. Because you and I are alike, united in guilt.'

When your friends act like this, they bind you to them more strongly than by any declaration of love.

But when your friends attack you and their aim isn't true, when they are aiming at other people (usually themselves) through you - that's to say, instead of looking at you, they are looking in the mirror - that's when your friends become terribly remote from you.

Édouard phones me back to say that there has been a misunderstanding and that I have misrepresented what he has said. He gently mocks the emphasis I put on our being friends, something I have done regularly over the nigh on fifteen years that we have known each other. We make up by having lunch in the little Italian restaurant at the entrance to the library where I work.

Édouard knew Françoise Sagan. He tells me the things he remembers about her – he does an imitation of how she used to answer the phone in a Spanish accent in order to weed out unwanted callers informing them that 'Madame Sagan is not in.' I say to him, 'You loved her so much, so I don't understand why you shouldn't be pleased that I – your friend – am writing a book about her.'

'Of course I'm pleased,' he replies, 'but that's not the problem. What annoys me is that you're abandoning your novel.'

Édouard is a generous soul, just as Françoise was.

So, for the last ten days roughly, whenever someone asks me, 'What are you up to at the moment? Are you writing anything?'

I answer, 'Yes, I'm writing a book about Françoise Sagan.'

Like a chemical reaction, people's initial response is always the same: it's as if a combination of certain words automatically produces a smile.

Utter the name 'Françoise Sagan' and you will see a smile come over people's faces, the same smile you would see if you were to say, 'Will you have some champagne?'

I am wondering whether, in agreeing to write about her, I am not going to put myself in an impossible position by touching on what belongs to everyone. All of a sudden I am afraid of this book.

Yesterday when I put a whole series of questions to Denis Westhoff (What perfume did she wear? What year was it that she met Pasolini? Where was her brother Jacques living in January 1954? etc.) he said something very important.

'My mother was never afraid.'

'Even in 1954, when she was just a young girl, before her first book came out, do you not think she was afraid?'

'No, she wasn't afraid of anything or anyone.'

'But she must have wondered whether she would get good reviews.'

'It was one of the things she taught me. Not to be afraid.'

I make a note in my work-book: 'A scene to show that Françoise Sagan was never afraid of anything.'

I make a note in my head: Must teach my daughter that the only thing to be afraid of is fear itself.

Clearly, in my hands, there is a danger that Françoise Sagan might be lost to view. I am appropriating her for myself, just as a portrait painter imposes his own profile on the portrait of the sitter.

I am going to slide her into my bed with its rumpled sheets, there to wipe away the anguished sweat that, though I attribute it to her, is so like mine. *She* may not be afraid, but I am. So I let my black hair intertwine with her fairness and, like a photographer using light-sensitive paper, I develop the outlines of a silhouette that, while grave, is full of joy. I can't help myself. If it's a problem, all anyone had to do was not to ask me in the first place.

It is 11 January 1954.

It is so cold outside that Marie Quoirez, Françoise's mother, has agreed to lend her daughter her fur coat, made from the silvery pelts of squirrels which, even after death, do not lose their ash-grey colour, while the belly remains as pale as Snow White's thigh. The fur coat is so big on Françoise that Marie pictures her daughter as she was eighteen years previously, a gift from heaven, a newborn baby wrapped in a blanket.

Jacques is expecting her to join him for dry martinis at the Hôtel Lutetia. In the taxi taking her across town, Françoise is deep in thought as she looks out of the window at the succession of illuminated signs adorning Haussmann's buildings: 'Frigeco', 'Paris-Pêcheur', 'Chocolat Suchard', 'Janique', 'Gevapan' and, especially, 'Grand Marnier', advertised in that Gothic script that makes you want to be sipping a liqueur in front of a log fire.

The taxi carrying Françoise drives alongside the courtyard of the Palais-Royal, as yet devoid of Buren's columns, then past the Louvre without the addition of the Pyramid and the Jardins du Carrousel without Maillol's bronze statues. By day Paris is sooty black. At night she is navy blue.

Françoise enters the Lutetia through the revolving doors, which muffle the noise from outside and give you the feeling of moving into a world wrapped in cotton wool. Her feet go trotting over the chequered marble floor of the luxury hotel. She recalls that, at the Liberation, a girl Jacques was engaged to at the time, Denise Franier, whose surname before the war had been Frankenstein, had been driving them through Paris in a mustard-coloured Rovin D4. As they passed the hotel she had told them it was there that whole families were awaiting the return of their fathers, mothers, brothers, sisters and children, and news from Poland and Germany.

Françoise has not forgotten those entire families that had disappeared. Even if she never referred to them, some things may be heard very clearly in the silence of their not being spoken about.

Comfortably ensconced in one of the deep red-velvet armchairs, sipping a cocktail, and paying no heed to the shrieks of laughter that pierce her heart like shards of glass, Françoise is not listening to her brother's friends, who are already drunk.

At that moment she is immersing herself in her memories.

The sharp, crystalline music of the tinkling ice cubes is taking her back to the war years.

She is seven.

Seven is old, so old that it is called 'the age of reason'.

She is living in the Isère, in Saint-Marcellin, at the foot of the mountains of the Vercors. The whole family has left

Paris because of the war; on the day of their departure they had to turn round and come back because Marie, the mother, had forgotten to collect her hats from the famous milliner's, Paulette's.[11]

Some weeks later, soldiers of the Wehrmacht come to search the house, which has the misfortune to be called 'The Gunnery'; they are looking for arms. They know that a van belonging to members of the Resistance has been spotted in the area. They get all the Quoirez family to line up and face the wall while they carry out the search. The story has a happy ending, as the Germans don't find anything.[12] But Françoise can remember the sound of her own breathing as, hands clasped on her head, she heard orders being given in a foreign tongue and the dogs barking. And she also remembers not being afraid.

I get the impression that for many French children of that generation, that is to say, those who were children during the war, their memories are not painful. Fear is not their abiding memory and the expression 'a long holiday' often crops up. Two things are mentioned: the women whose hair was shorn for having fraternised with the enemy and the revelation of images from the death camps. When you come to think of it, it is rather strange that an awareness of the war should be defined by those two things, both of which date from the period after the war, and yet they are cited in answer to the question 'What do you remember about the war?'

This is what Françoise remembers: she was eleven when she went to the cinema in Saint-Marcellin to see *In Old Chicago*, an American film starring Tyrone Power. It was 1946 and newsreels were shown before the film started. Suddenly there appeared on the screen those images of Buchenwald and Auschwitz in which you see snow ploughs clearing away heaps of corpses. It took Françoise some time, a few seconds at least, to realise what she was seeing.[13]

A friend of mine, Gérard Rambert, once told me that when he discovered some photographs under his parents' radiator cover, all he could see in them were hills. He could not understand why his parents would hide 'photographs of hills' in their radiators. It had taken him several days to realise what it was all about. Just as the faces in the paintings of Arcimboldo are made up of vegetables or fruit, so the hills in the photographs belonging to Gérard's parents were made up of bones and decomposed corpses.

In *Un Pedigree*, Patrick Modiano would write, 'At the age of thirteen I discovered the images of the death camps. Something changed for me that day.'

Those two sentences say it all.

'Something changed for me that day' is an experience that we have all had, every one of us, whatever our age or culture and whatever generation we belong to.

I remember the day when something changed for me.

I must have been six or seven.

My mother placed a big history book on the baize surface of her writing desk. We pored over its pages. I don't think I realised at first what I was seeing – I'm not talking about its meaning or import, I am merely saying that it was difficult to work out what the photographs were of.

My mother explained to me that we belonged to that family of bodies, that we were 'Jews'.

'Something changed for me that day.'

If I mention all these things, in a digression that is taking me further than I intended, it is because I see in Françoise Sagan's levity, in her irreverence and offhandedness, not an elegant front concealing despair, but a sign of her secret awareness of human suffering. She had no legitimate right to speak of suffering, for she belonged neither with the victims nor indeed with the executioners. Françoise Sagan was never to tire of exploring forms of distress that may be regarded as merely trivial but I sense that there was a deeply embedded seriousness in Françoise Quoirez that she respected too much to make it her own. And I know that the sight of a shaven-headed woman paraded through the streets of the village where she, Françoise, lived as a child was to haunt her for the rest of her days.[14]

'So, what's this about you waiting to hear back from publishers?'

Françoise, put on the spot by a friend who is flirting with her brother Jacques, comes out of her daydream.

'Yes, well, we'll see,' she replies, pushing back a lock of hair that has fallen forward.

'So,' insists someone else, 'have you heard back?'

Few things make Françoise feel more ill at ease. She doesn't want to talk about it. She is furious with her brother and his big mouth.

'No, not yet. I only dropped the manuscript off last week … it can take several months.'

This is the cue for people to give their opinions, to come up with an anecdote about someone who had been read by Gide for Gallimard, or someone else who received a letter with a positive reply, or Proust who paid to have his work published, and so on and so on. Françoise has had enough. She doesn't want to have to listen to them any more; she feels dizzy.

It's at this point that her friend Véronique whispers to her, 'Come with me, I'll take you to the carnival. We'll have our fortunes told.'

The two girls grab their coats, then hail a beetle-black Citroën taxi on Boulevard Raspail.

'We're going to Pigalle,' says Véronique, in the serious voice she reserves for special occasions.

So here are the girls, speeding through the night towards their future. It's not the first time that Françoise has met a fortune-teller. The previous year, in Rue l'Abbé-Groult, a blonde woman with an enormous bosom had announced to her, 'You will write a book that will cross the oceans'[15] and that had encouraged her to take from her drawer the few pages that had been lying there abandoned.

So it all stemmed from the woman who had predicted that Françoise would write books and that they would be very successful.

I can't see into the future, but I do have one extraordinary power, the power to transport Françoise back to that night in Pigalle.

Up there on the heights, from mid-December until mid-January, a carnival with dozens of strange booths sets up along Boulevard Rochechouart, stretching from Place Blanche to the Anvers Métro station. There you can find women who will tell your fortune with playing cards, as well as shooting galleries, bearded ladies and fishing for prizes.

I quote here from the photographer Christer Strömholm, who photographed these carnivals in the late fifties:[16]

You could get to see wrestling matches … Dwarves with beards would invite you to performances that lasted an hour.

The female snake charmer in her glass case would allow big, lazy snakes to coil languorously round her body. You had to pay to see her. We would watch in fascination for a good quarter of an hour.

Her working day was long and whenever she took a break she would leave her glass case but she never parted from her snakes. They stayed tightly coiled round her half-naked body. There was always a packed house for the 'leopard woman'. She would let us stroke her hairy patches.

I can imagine Françoise and Véronique wandering among the stalls and the roundabouts. I can see them laughing at the dodgems, sinking their teeth into round, sweet toffee-apples and getting candyfloss moustaches as they stood guffawing in front of the booth of the crocodile woman – half woman, half crocodile.

I like to picture them, complete with the leather handbags that mark them out as well-brought-up young ladies, entering the fortune-teller's booth.

There are some grey and orange stones on the fortune-teller's table; light from the candles throws into relief the wrinkles on her face – she could be one hundred years old – she wears jewellery, lots of jewellery. She asks Françoise to choose some cards and place them on the table, then she stands up, takes a pendulum and, looking Françoise straight in the eye, says to her in a gravelly voice that conjures up some never-never land, 'I see someone who is coming to live with you, someone who will be arriving in the near future.

'It's someone you will get to know very well indeed, someone you will love and who will love you straight away, for you are very lovable. But, beware, the relationship between you will be one of extremes for she is haughty and capricious. She will love you as children love, unreasonably. She will love you as women love: if you neglect them, they do not easily forgive.

'This is someone you will know for the rest of your life, who will at times desert you and then you will suffer greatly. As she brushes past, you will always call her name. You must honour and cherish her, for you are one of those who know how to make her happy. You know how to make her laugh and to entertain her. She is on her way towards you. And when you open the door to her, you must look her straight in the face.'

'Who is this person?'

'It is Lady Luck.'[17]

My first paid job was as a reader for a publishing house. So I know all about manuscripts and what peculiar, repugnant, necessary, exciting things they are, inviting contempt and consideration in equal measure. I know the mystique surrounding those pages, those accumulating piles. I am familiar with the disillusionment and sadness that come from reading words that are just not right, that are as indigestible as food which doesn't taste as it should. But sometimes, too, you feel your temples begin to throb and walls come tumbling down, when you read words that make a deep impression on you and help you to go on living.

Readers in publishing houses are a strange breed, somewhat wan, somewhat apart, somewhat feared; because the talent they have, their possessing 'a good eye' (in the same way as a person is said to 'have a nose' for things) is a gift: it's a type of expertise that cannot be either passed on or explained – it's as scary as witchcraft.

These are creatures wreathed in a slightly malodorous aura who loiter alone in the corridors with sheets of paper and folders under their arm, and such a one was François Le Grix, the reader at the publishing house of René Julliard in 1954.

He was nicknamed 'Grixe' or 'the Grey Lady' and, on account of that ridiculous moniker, I imagine him to be a tall, slender, colourless individual, made fun of by the others for wearing 'a toupee which only he thought was undetectable'.[18]

François Le Grix is the first reader of *Bonjour Tristesse* on that thirteenth of January 1954.

Conscientious as ever, before he finishes his work for the day, in his fine hand – the handwriting of a schoolboy brought up under the Third Republic, who knows all his *sous-préfectures* by heart and can solve problems involving trains that pass one another – he writes this:

What Mademoiselle Quoirez has penned bowls along nicely without faltering. Hence we are prevented from noticing the numerous barbarisms that it would be appropriate to eradicate from such a pleasing text. In the very first line, I light upon the following: 'To this strange feeling … I hesitate to apply the fine name of sadness.' Not only does it lack euphony but the syntax also offends … At one point the author writes of 'the hearing of that exaggerated laughter' instead of 'hearing that laughter'. I have underlined many of these infelicities, which the exercise of a little care would suffice to correct. The charm of the work, the rather particular spell it casts, produced by its mix of perversion and innocence, stems also from a complacent attitude to life being coupled with bitterness towards it, and from gentleness being coupled with cruelty. In places it is a poem as much as a novel, but without there being any break in tone or any false note sounded. Above all, it is a novel where life is depicted authentically and where the psychology, for all that it is daring, cannot be faulted, since its five characters, Raymond, Cécile, Anne, Elsa and Cyril, are boldly drawn and not to be forgotten in a hurry. The style of writing is in essence so classical that in quite a few instances the imperfect subjunctive would flow more naturally than the present subjunctive, which is rarely the case. But Mademoiselle Quoirez persists in not using it. Another example of a barbarism, and a rather curious one, concerns the book's actual title, inspired by its final lines, where the author tells us that, with the advent of evening, a strange face appears to her which she greets with the words 'Bonjour tristesse'. In that it is evening, would it not be better to say 'Bonsoir tristesse' and, furthermore, would not the title gain thereby?[19]

As if clinging to a talisman, I have retained all the reports I wrote when I was a reader. They are in a big grey box file which I keep archived in the bedroom I had as a child in my parents' house. I would like to reread them all, one day. In amongst them is a report on a first novel that went on to be a great success. It had been written by a girl of my own age – twenty at the time – and I had been greatly struck when reading it. It was the first time I had read a manuscript that seemed to me to be undeniably both well written and likely to sell. So I had spoken up for it to the publisher, for whom I was working as an intern.

Some years later, at a dimly lit Parisian party, I ran across that same girl, who was now famous on account of her book. I was then working in a theatre on the Champs-Élysées. Needless to say, we were still both the same age as each other. But the success of her book had catapulted her into what seemed to me to be life as it was meant to be lived, whereas I was vegetating in the limbo of my own mere existence. I asked her for a light, and she obliged, but in an offhand way, without even bothering to look at me, so as not to lose the thread of the animated discourse with which she was regaling her male audience.

I said to myself, 'You're not looking at me and you don't know who I am. Yet I was one of the fairies present round your cradle.'

I often think of that incident.

In doing so, I wonder which of the people who cross my path, their faces unknown to me, have nonetheless played a part in my life without my being the slightest bit aware of it.

What I find striking in the story of Françoise Sagan is that the fairies who were present round that little girl's cradle, all those capricious fairy godmothers – *toutes les capricieuses mères du destin* – in whose hands her destiny lay and who played their part in the making of her fame, were all very elderly gentlemen.

First there was François Le Grix, then Pierre Javet and René Julliard, the publishing house trio. Next up were Mauriac, Blanchot, Paulhan, Bataille and then many others, a whole Senate's worth of wonderful old men who covered their faces in dainty veils to grant the wish of a girl-child newly born.

But we are not yet at that point. We are still just at the point where the reader's report from François Le Grix lands on the desk of Pierre Javet, editorial director at the publishing house of René Julliard, who, in turn, is shortly to be overcome with stupefaction (in the etymological sense of the word).

Before I recount what happened on the night of 16–17 January 1954, the night René Julliard read the manuscript of *Bonjour Tristesse* for the first time and wanted to publish it before he had even reached the last page, I must describe something that happened to me yesterday. It was such a strange thing that I wonder if I really did experience it, so strange that I could not say exactly what was going on.

I had decided to make an appointment with a clairvoyant, because, after I had written the episode with the fortune-teller, I reckoned that for me to meet a 'real' clairvoyant would be useful for the book and would make my description a bit less kitsch.

There are two sorts of writers. There are those who plumb their own depths to extract all the black gold they can find there and who, for that reason, are forced to live a life of asceticism. And there are those who need to experience things in order to write about them and who lose their way as they journey through life on the edge of a fantasy world, obliged to lead a kind of existence that sometimes proves fatal to them, as the wild ass's skin does to the hero in Balzac's story.

Be that as it may, I had made an appointment with the clairvoyant using the book as a pretext even though, probably, at an unconscious level, I wanted just as much to hear things about my personal life: my separation from the father of my daughter was looking as if it might be permanent and never in my life had I felt quite as lost as I did then. But instead of speaking to her about that, I put the following question: 'I am writing a book at the moment. Can you see it?' This is what I asked the clairvoyant when I met her in her studio near the Anvers Métro station, which in the fifties was the exact location – and I am not making this up – of the Pigalle carnival.

(What I am going to write next is the exact transcription of the notes I scribbled down in the course of our conversation. I am reproducing the words just as they were said to me, without any attempt to dress them up stylistically or to impose any kind of coherence on them after the event.

I know that most readers will not for one moment accept the veracity of what I am going to report. Yet it is all true and I leave it to each individual to interpret as they wish, and as best they can, the remarkable occurrence that I was party to and that I restrict myself here to conveying as faithfully as possible.)

'Yes, I can see that you are writing a book on someone's life. It's the life of a woman who lived as a man would. She was very masculine. But she was benevolent towards people. She was a woman who had experienced everything. She did whatever she wanted to do. But she did it alone. She experienced everything on her own.

'She was a woman who felt misunderstood. She had stepped aside from time. For her there was no longer any such thing as a calendar, only a life lived in the present moment.

'Françoise Sagan.

'I am seeing Françoise Sagan – that's correct, isn't it?

'From beyond the grave, she is wondering why society wished to destroy her. She is asking herself that question, she is asking you that question. Just like a tsunami, just as when the sea comes up and lays waste to everything, so society took everything back from her. Why?

'It was not she who self-destructed. They *truly* wished to kill her.

'She is trying to understand why she went from being an idol to a woman who was hated.

'It wasn't the writer they resented, but the person she was. They claimed back everything they had given her.

'Society took back from her what she had received. She wonders why. She is saying that perhaps it is because she herself repudiated what she symbolised in society.

'She repudiated her origins, the kind of world she came from. With the result that that world itself – those who had lauded her to the skies – repudiated her.

'She is asking you whether it was because it never occurred to her to say thank you. But as far as she was concerned, things were just "normal". Everything that happened to her was normal; she didn't understand that there was a payback involved.

'Now, we live in a society where you're not supposed to find it "normal" to receive so much money. You have to constantly say thank you and justify yourself and show gratitude.

'It didn't occur to her to say thank you, nor to tell anyone that she loved them.

'She could say to someone she met in the street, "Do you need a car? Here, take mine." But, in truth, she was not someone who gave. People believed that she felt nothing towards anyone and perhaps that was true. Perhaps she was fundamentally incapable of loving. Everything she was disintegrated.

'The reason lies in the soul of the person.

'She says, "Brigitte Bardot also lived a selfish life. But then she decided to speak up for animals, so people are touched by that. They recognise that she is doing something for others."

'She herself had no wish to pursue that kind of thing. Her view was that she had a right to do what she wanted with her own money.

'She is saying, "Maybe it's to do with my origins, right at the beginning." She hopes you will find the answer.

'She always thought she wasn't the person she was meant to be. She had to play a role.'

(Suddenly the clairvoyant looks at me, and speaks to me as if she were a doctor giving me a prescription at the end of the consultation.)

'You are sometimes going to want to do certain things that you are not used to doing. You will want to drink – go ahead. Drink alcohol.

'You have nothing to fear, she is watching over you and will know how to protect you. She is full of benevolence towards you. But be careful. You will want to smoke. Don't go in too much for cigarettes. She smoked to the point of suffocation. She virtually asphyxiated herself. On the other hand, you can drink, and may your drinking make her tipsy. Let yourself go. Let yourself be guided by her, guided towards liberty. You will have no regrets and you will never feel ashamed.

'She will help you grow. She will make a free woman of you.

'She will teach you. Let her enjoy some final moments through you.'

I reread these lines; they may seem grotesque.

I have nothing further to add to this episode. Miracles are not things you believe in: they are things you register when they happen. I can simply state that, before we met, the woman who spoke those words had read neither *Bonjour Tristesse* nor any biography of Françoise Sagan. And even if she had done extensive searches on the internet, she had no way of knowing that I was in the process of writing this book.

But let's move on, let's forget about that strange episode and return to the exceptionally cold weather of 16 January 1954, for the publisher René Julliard is dining in town at the home of Émile Roche, the President of the Economic Council.

Tall, elegant, his deep-set eyes accentuated by thick glasses with tortoiseshell frames, Julliard is a man in a hurry who has bagged three Goncourt prizes since the end of the war. His colleague, Robert Laffont, says of him, 'He adores receptions, he loves mixing with the glitterati and dining out, and this natural gregariousness of his is a great asset in terms of business, because on the one hand it gives him access to a huge array of works-in-progress while on the other hand providing him with tactical openings in his dealings with the press and literary panels. He created his publishing house in his own image: it is flexible, it is nimble and it sees itself as being up with the latest fashion.'[20]

The subject of conversation round the table this evening is

the ceremony of the transfer of powers between Vincent Auriol and the new French President, René Coty, which has just taken place this very day at the Élysée Palace.

Naturally, any talk of the new President focuses above all on the topic of his wife. Michelle Auriol, the previous First Lady of France, had style and posed for *Paris Match* in designer outfits. She was the kind of president's wife that the French go mad for: she was the daughter of working-class parents and had been in the Resistance during the war so, as well as having proletarian credentials, she had given proof of courage and, at the same time, with her elegance and her outfits, she had what it took to delight foreign heads of state. How important it is to French men and women for our First Lady to be attractive: we appreciate that quality far more highly than all the others put together, even more highly than moral qualities.

The problem as the press sees it in January 1954 is that Germaine Coty, the wife of the new President, in comparison with her predecessor, is like a Normandy cow.[21] It was in the coarse garb of convent schools that her body developed, hence she is mannish and seemingly untouched since birth by any trace of femininity.

On this, 16 January, the day on which power has been transferred to the incoming President, the French are furious that the new First Lady of France looks as if she's at some family bash, receiving journalists in the flour-bespattered clothes she has been cooking in. But, fortunately, the French do so love to love those they formerly hated (and vice versa) that they will very soon end up adoring this nice, fat lady and they will love her like one of those big chocolate logs you get at

Christmas, for her genuine kindness and her generosity.

After that topic has been well and truly chewed over, along with the *quenelles de brochet sauce financière*, the guests will most likely have discussed what had happened the day before at the Marigny Theatre. Everyone who was anyone in Paris had descended on it to discover for themselves the sound of 'avant-garde music' – Cocteau had even had to sit on the floor in front of the first row to hear Bach, Nono, Stockhausen, Webern and Stravinsky – as featured on the programme of a concert given by the young Pierre Boulez.

It is also likely, very likely even, that, between the *canetons façon Tour d'Argent* and the *pommes soufflées*, there will have been a quivering of moustaches at René Julliard's mention of a study by Dr Kinsey, just published within the previous few days, *Sexual Behavior in the Human Female*, an exploration of the female body that brings in 'the notion of pleasure'. And it is all based on 'practical observation'. No doubt there is some choking over the *salade mimosa* when René Julliard adds that he has been working with the writer Daniel Guérin on a book entitled *Le Rapport Kinsey*, a French analysis of this new approach to female sexuality.

And, again, it is likely that conversation will have dwelt for a time on the winner of the top award in French cinema, Claude Autant-Lara, for his adaptation of Colette's novel *The Ripening Seed*.

In Paris a coalition for the defence of moral and social values has written an open letter to the director, cautioning him thus: 'We disliked your plan for a film based on Colette's work because of the damaging moral repercussions such a film would inevitably have on the young people of our country as a whole.'

Did these shades, reunited here around the dinner table, make mention of the violent demonstrations taking place against the Syrian regime? Or of the clashes between the Muslim Brotherhood and militants of the Liberation Rally founded by Nasser in Egypt? Or did they speak of that resolution of the United Nations Security Council, the aim of which was 'to achieve progress towards lasting peace in Palestine: it is essential that the parties abide strictly by their obligations under the General Armistice Agreement of 20 July 1949 between Syria and Israel'.

That is less likely. But, really, what does it matter? What matters for us is that, this evening, René Julliard is in a state of exhilaration, having been intoxicated by the Grands-Échezeaux 1938 served at table, and that the sparkling conversation has so sharpened his senses that, on returning home, the words 'Colette', 'sexual behaviour of women' and 'avant-garde music' are ringing in his ears and putting him in a particular mood. In just the same way, certain beliefs maintain that the position of the planets in the sky determines the character of a baby at the moment of its birth.

The moment the twelve strokes of midnight ring out from the gilded brass pendulum enclosed in its glass case, René Julliard decides not to go to bed straight away but to stay up and read for a while.

As if removing it from its corolla of petals, he takes the manuscript that François Le Grix and Pierre Javet have recommended out of its daffodil-yellow folder.

'Françoise Quoirez, 167 Boulevard Malesherbes. Carnot 59-61. Date of birth: 21 June 1935.'

René Julliard does some rapid mental arithmetic: the little girl is still a minor, so it will be all raindrops on roses, nothing that will require too much effort on his part, he hopes, after a dinner at which the wine has flowed so copiously.

His mind automatically goes to one of his favourite books, *The Girls*, by Henry de Montherlant. It brings a smile to his lips and he gets out of his armchair to fetch from the bookcase that delightfully misogynistic work – he rejoices at every reading of it.

> Young girls are like stray dogs. If you look on them with the slightest hint of benevolence they think you are calling them and that you are going to rescue them, and they paw friskily at your trousers.[22]

Would his evening not be better spent reading Montherlant rather than the scribblings of some little poppet?

René Julliard lays the manuscript at his feet and searches his shelves for *The Girls*, but in vain. For some reason they have disappeared, so our publisher is obliged to take up the first page of the manuscript with that peculiar title: *Bonjour Tristesse*.

To this strange feeling of mine, obsessing me with its sweet languor, I hesitate to apply the fine, solemn name of sadness.

It takes René Julliard several attempts to read the first sentence because mentally he is not quite prepared, his thoughts still quite distracted by the dinner he has been at. In an effort to concentrate, to focus, he blows his nose, then clears his throat. Openings are so difficult to get right, he muses, especially when it's a first novel. They can often be over-egged or consciously understated, like girls wearing too much make-up who aim at an immediately pleasing effect, unaware that the most charming thing of all is to be attractive without trying.

To this strange feeling of mine, obsessing me with its sweet languor, I hesitate to apply the fine, solemn name of sadness.

The intoxication from the meal has affected René Julliard's vision, so the lines are running into one another before his very eyes. Reading the first sentence again one last time, he all of a sudden sees the beauty in it, with the result that he immediately sobers up.

To this strange feeling of mine, obsessing me with its sweet languor, I hesitate to apply the fine, solemn name of sadness.

Straight away his heart is trapped between the lines of the book – he cannot say whether it is beating faster or whether it has stopped beating. Before he knows what has happened, he has devoured the first half of the novel, dumbfounded by this young girl – she talks like an old man who has seen all there is to see, has read all there is to read, has experienced everything, and she is able to write, 'I did not like young people,' while even depicting her father as if he were a lover. 'I cannot imagine a better or more amusing friend … I knew his need for women.'

What René Julliard feels is like a surge of electricity in his blood radiating through his entire body, the feeling you have when you launch yourself forward on a swing with your head thrown back.

All this time, within his own head, several different men have been summoned, for each in turn to read the words of the book through a single pair of eyes. Within one man, several are assembled. First of all there is 'the reader', the man who can appreciate how a sentence is created through the life breathed into it by lines constructed round a ternary rhythm which, as in music, is a strong rhythm yet one that the author can interrupt without warning, with the precision of a great conductor, one of those truly gifted conductors who can render all trace of effort invisible. 'I was greatly attracted to the concept of love affairs that were rapidly embarked upon, intensely experienced and quickly over. At the age I was, fidelity held no attraction. I knew little of love, apart from its trysts, its kisses and its lethargies.' Next comes 'the publisher' to supplant 'the reader': it is he now who begins to read these lines, all of a sudden wondering what the author of these pages might be like in the flesh, and anxious to know if the story is wholly autobiographical or if, on the contrary, it is fictionalised: 'My father, whether from inclination or habit, liked to dress me up as a "femme fatale".' At times the publisher loses his way, he forgets his role, and then it is simply 'the man' who takes his place and begins to read through eyes that are popping out, so affected is he by those words, which can only have been written by either a virgin or a very experienced woman – here the two seem to have miraculously melded, like some Frankenstein's monster made up of different sorts of women, the resulting creation capable of saying, without naivety or dissimulation, 'You are the most handsome man I know.'

On reading these words, Julliard straightens up from the waist, a considerable length, and rises, like a stork abruptly unfolding its long, black wings before it flaps off. Impatiently he pushes back his tartan rug, gets a foot tangled up in it, shakes off his shoe to free himself, then rushes over to his desk, one of those substantial English desks in solid wood overlaid with dark mahogany and leather-topped. René Julliard pulls open every one of its drawers and, in so doing, causes his forelock to flop down over his tortoiseshell glasses but he does not even pause to push it back, so intent is he on finding a pencil to use for annotating the manuscript. All of a sudden he takes on the boyish look of a student just out of bed, tousle-headed and having to put on his spectacles before he can see properly.

In vain René searches for a charcoal pencil so that he can begin noting in places the comments he will need to share with Javet, Le Grix and the author; for it's settled, there will be no procrastinating, the book will be published as quickly as possible; ringing in his ears are the words: 'His kissing became serious. It quickly became urgent and skilful, too skilful ... It was dawning on me that I was better suited to kissing a boy in the sun than to studying for a degree.' René Julliard curses the tiny pair of bird-shaped scissors that have just pricked his finger at the bottom of the drawer, but eventually he finds a pencil. Just as it is inconceivable that you would tear yourself away from the embrace of a woman whom you are covering from head to toe in kisses, so it is equally inconceivable that he would put a book down in order to perform some extraneous task. René Julliard rushes back to the manuscript in a panic, as if the words he has just read could have been effaced by a magic sponge, and here he is at last, bundled up in the tartan rug and holding the pages of the manuscript. The words are still there, they send a warm glow through his whole body; in the end they will become completely intoxicating: 'I had always heard love being spoken of as something quite straightforward. I had myself spoken of it crudely, with the ignorance of youth, but it seemed to me now that I would never again be able to speak of it in that way, in that detached and coarse manner.'

At daybreak, Gisèle d'Assailly, a descendant of General La Fayette, found her husband asleep in an armchair with a hundred pages scattered around him.

Gisèle stooped to bring some order to all those loose sheets, causing her husband to wake with a sudden start.

'But it doesn't add up!' he exclaimed.

It was Gisèle's turn to be startled.

Overnight the alcoholic haze in René Julliard's head had dispersed and all had again become clear: it was impossible for a child of eighteen to have written those lines. Viewed as a mathematical equation, it didn't add up, for a girl capable of handling the language so perfectly and depicting so accurately the habits of the bourgeoisie could not but belong to that same class herself.

Now, what bourgeois family would allow a slip of a girl to have the following exchange with her father?

'Sleep well, did you?' my father asked.

'So-so,' I replied. 'I drank too much whisky last night.'

What kind of parents could give their offspring an upbringing that, from a cultural standpoint, was beyond reproach, while at the same time encouraging her to lose her virginity, like some slut, on the beach?

No, it simply didn't stand up.

Virtually bellowing, René Julliard ordered his wife to assist him in getting up from the chair he had nodded off in and to help him to the telephone (which actually had a room of its own, called 'the telephone room'), since the uncomfortable position he had slept in had made him go numb and had restricted his circulation to such an extent that he was unable to support himself on his own two legs.

Because his hands had seized up, he asked Gisèle to dial the automatic telephone exchange so that he could speak directly to the mysterious author hiding behind a girl's name. What's more, wasn't the exactness of the date of birth on the manuscript's folder itself proof that someone was trying to get the better of him? They were trying to lay a trap for him.

But who could in fact be hiding behind that pseudonym 'Françoise Quoirez'? It was a man, of that he was sure. Perhaps it was quite simply the father of the girl and she was being sent as a decoy to entice him. In any case, the man had to be in his middle years to be capable of depicting so very exactly the character of a beautiful woman growing old: 'Being forty must bring with it the fear of loneliness, perhaps the last stirrings of desire … Probably at her age I'll also be paying young men to love me, because love is the sweetest thing, it's what in life is most vivid and has the most point. So the price paid hardly matters.'

How, even for a moment, could he have believed that a girl who was still a minor could have written those lines? How could he have thought of basing the promotion of the book on the youthfulness of the author? He would have laughed at himself and at his gullibility as a publisher ready to believe anything, if he had not felt rather ashamed. Meanwhile his wife, her still dishevelled hair forming a spray of feathers that waggled on her skull, was handing him the receiver.

'Hello, this is René Julliard speaking, of Éditions René Julliard. Is that the home of Mademoiselle Quoirez?'

'To whom exactly do you wish to speak?' asked Julia, who was not accustomed to elderly men phoning for Françoise, and most certainly not at such an early hour on a Sunday morning.

'I would like to speak to Françoise Quoirez,' he repeated, pronouncing each syllable distinctly.

'I'm afraid you can't. She's asleep at this hour of the morning. And I've been instructed on no account to wake her.'

'Very good, thank you,' replied René Julliard, before hanging up.

This strange response merely confirmed his suspicions. What kind of French family was it that allowed girls to sleep on when they should have been at mass, or doing physical jerks, or breakfasting with the family?

How could both Javet and Le Grix have failed to voice the slightest doubt as to the author's identity? They were either very stupid or very naïve. No matter, he was going to lay a trap for whoever it was that had set out to trap him. No one was going to hoodwink the man who had published three Goncourt prize-winners in a row.

Jean-Jacques Gautier in 1946.

Jean-Louis Curtis in 1947.

And Maurice Druon in 1948.

René Julliard is making arrangements.

He has a telegram sent to the home of the Sleeping Beauty and asks his secretary if she will travel in specially on a Sunday for the occasion: they will welcome the young girl appropriately even though she is being served up as bait for him to swallow. In the meantime he is going to think up a series of questions with Le Grix, designed to flush out whoever is wielding the fishing hook baited with childish charms.

'Oh, at last,' says Françoise to herself, when she finds the telegram lying next to her bowl of warm milky coffee.

Meeting today 5 p.m. at Éditions René Julliard.

*

She had never doubted that a reply would come soon, but she had been wondering how many more days she would have to wait. As she bit into her buttered bread with honey – to begin with, it pushes her mouth out of shape and gets wedged against her palate, then the honey mixes with the butter to form a nectar that trickles into the bread, softening it as far as the crust – Françoise, her eyes closed, worked out the number of days. Eleven. She had waited eleven days for a reply regarding publication and in her view that was acceptable. As always, things happened just at the moment when you were no longer thinking about them, for all you have to do is to give up wishing for something, ignore it for a while, and eventually, annoyed at no longer being wished for, it comes to you.

At around 3 p.m., while Françoise was concocting some vague story to persuade her father to lend her his black Buick, René Julliard was climbing the stairs to the sixth floor of his publishing house to see François Le Grix, who lived there.

Le Grix loved his attic room, for it made him like the character from *Les Misérables*, Marius, the baron, who opted for study and poverty rather than for gilded surroundings and chandeliers, and who would read at night by the light of a candle, happier there than in the Hall of Mirrors at the Palace of Versailles. Whereas his colleagues wondered about the parsimonious existence he led and considered his everyday routine to be grey and monotonous, François Le Grix was able to cast himself as the hero of his own life story – an ability that brings happiness to all those who possess it.

Françoise Quoirez arrived at 5 p.m. on the dot.

No one knows exactly what transpired during the three hours of discussion between the girl and her publisher.

Three hours is a long time for people who don't know each other. Of course, just as I have imagined the hours that led up to what, in the history of literature, ranks as a legendary meeting, so too I could invent the questions put and answers given. But the hours are passing, as are the days, and I really must move forward through the year 1954, for I have only reached the middle of January. It is a month and a half since I began work on this book and I still have so many things to write.

Let us not therefore dwell on what was said. The upshot was that when he left his office René Julliard expressed no doubt as to the writer of the work: that strange young girl, sharp-witted as a fox, was indeed the author of *Bonjour Tristesse*. He had discovered a writer, had asked her how much she wanted as an advance and she had called his bluff with the figure she threw out.

'Twenty-five thousand francs.'

He had replied, 'Fine, I'm offering you twice that,' which certainly pleased Françoise who, on rejoining Florence in the Café de l'Espérance, announced proudly, 'We'll buy a Jaguar with the money from the book!'

Florence Malraux, when I met her in her apartment in Rue de l'Université yesterday afternoon, stressed the word 'we'.

I got there far too early; it's a habit of mine, one that

Parisians find so annoying and provincial. Consequently I had to kick my heels for roughly ten minutes on the ground floor of her apartment block, before going up four floors to where she lives.

For the first time in my life as an author I was going to meet, in the flesh, a 'character' from a book, for hitherto I had had knowledge of Florence only through the biographies of Françoise Sagan and from the book by her cousin, Alain Malraux, which I had perused the day before in the André Malraux Library in order to prepare for my interview with her as thoroughly as possible.

After I have waited for the time of the appointment to come round and walked up four flights because I don't trust lifts, Florence Malraux comes to open her door to me. I am immediately impressed by her. Gentle in aspect, with intelligent, kindly eyes that are full of merriment, she is just as I have imagined from everything I have managed to read about her, all the descriptions given by those who have been lucky enough to know her personally.

In the drawing room where we sit together there are books, books everywhere, and the reproduction of a painting of a swimming pool by David Hockney, its colours slightly faded by the sun.

'I remember the first time I met Françoise at the Cours Hattemer; she was wearing a green coat. Because we were physically alike, people often assumed we were sisters. She was a little younger than me and she was the first person who ever asked me specific questions about my life during the war. And questions about the Resistance. She was unique, she wasn't like other people. She had an intensity that came from her expression and an awareness of the sky and clouds. We used to go for walks in Paris and together we experienced moments of pure poetry. I think that we believed in our lucky star. At least, she believed in it enough for both of us. I remember her father giving us money to go and have dinner at Lipp's. He took out rolls of banknotes, which impressed me. He adored being with his daughter and his daughter's friends. He was a whimsical sort of person who loved playing games: one day he served us breakfast in bed dressed up as a maid! You know, it was a funny time to be a girl. We were not allowed to wear trousers or make-up. I even remember that at the Lycée Fénelon we had to have our hands inspected as we went in, for the staff to check that our fingernails were clean. In those days there was no contraception. Accidents did happen. If you were rich, you went to Switzerland. But for the poor it was more complicated and also more risky. I remember that, on several occasions, we helped girls in the office. It was 1954, which was when I started work at Gallimard. They would come in and collapse and they needed help. Françoise would manage to get some money together – she got it from her family and then, later on, it was her own money – and someone would accompany the girls, often to the outskirts of Paris.

'Françoise was always willing to come to people's aid, she always helped others. We told no one, not even our parents.

'When we met, at the age of sixteen, Françoise was already finding that life was moving too slowly for her liking. She knew that she would be a writer. She had no doubt that she would earn her living by writing books. When she came out of her first meeting with Julliard, she said to me, "We'll buy a Jaguar with the money from the book!" She said "we" because she did not consider that things belonged just to her. Her greatest pleasure was to share her life.'

I explain to Florence that my book is taking on a strange form, somewhere between a novel, a biography and a fictionalised autobiography. I tell her, therefore, that she will feature in it significantly and that I hope she will agree to be a character of mine, for I would like this book to talk more than anything else about friendship. That is probably because, at the point where I am in my life, stories about friends are of much more interest to me than love stories. I feel unable to speak of Françoise Sagan's love affairs. I find it impossible to put myself in the frame of mind of someone in love.

I say, 'I get the impression that in 1954, even if, as the evidence of her book shows, her thoughts dwell a lot on physical love, friendship is the really important thing. What's more, once she has become successful she is going to gather a group of friends around her – Jacques Chazot, Michel Magne, Bernard Frank, Charlotte Aillaud, Nicole Wisniak, Véronique Campion, Frédéric Botton, Juliette Gréco, Annabel Buffet ... – long before meeting a "husband". I want to talk about friendship, for I take a jaundiced view of love relationships, whereas I do believe that, if I had not met my female friends, I would not be the woman I am today. I'm not saying that I would have been the worse for it; I might have been all the better for it – who knows? But what I can state is that my life would have been quite different. It is as if today we bear responsibility for one another, for we have each played an active part in shaping the other person. Love is different. Love is something you live through and that lives through you, but I do not believe that, at any deep level, it makes us who we are.'

Florence smiles that smile of hers, as gentle as her name, and I am relieved, for to me, at the point where I am in writing this book, she is like the priestess of the oracle at Delphi; she *knows*.

I talk to her about Virginia Woolf's book, which her mother translated and which I have included in my depiction of the teenage Françoise's room.

'Do you think that in 1954 Françoise might have had *A Room of One's Own* on her bedside table? I've seen that it was translated by your mother.'

'That's right, my mother did translate it, but I don't think people read Virginia Woolf until quite a bit later. In 1954 we were reading Proust, Dostoyevsky ... but Woolf, I don't think so.'

'Oh, that's a pity. I thought it might be a good idea, because it would make the link with you and with your mother.'

'Well then, put it in her room! What does it matter?'

'Oh, I don't want to write things that aren't true.'

'You know, Anne, what counts is that you should write things that ring true.'

Looking at Florence Malraux, I say to myself that I would really love to be like her, later on. Of course, it's stupid to say 'later on'. I would really love to be like her now. Does one write in order to be someone else? I wonder. Very probably. I would have really loved to be Françoise Sagan and to have written an amazing book at the age of eighteen. I would have loved to drink, to love, to drive, to have fun and to drink again. But I am only who I am, and I have failed my driving test four times. Anyway, I prefer to travel by train.

'Since you are now my character, you have to give your approval for me to go on. You must read the beginning and be happy with it.'

When I get back home I slip the first ten pages into an envelope.

As I contemplate the yellow postbox, I cross my fingers.

Françoise too closes her eyes when she thinks of Florence.

With Florence at her side she has the exhilarating sense that she is someone worthy of being read and listened to. She often thinks of the life her friend led during the war. Or, rather, the non-life, a life of flight and persecution. She must ask her to tell the story once again of how, with her mother Clara Malraux, née Goldschmidt, they slept in a firemen's barracks in Toulouse and then in a cellar. There was no heating, no food. A young man of nineteen, Edgar Nahoum, steals grains of rice for them in shops, out of pity for the starving little girl. He slips a few grains between his fingers and then into his pocket. It's better than nothing. After the war he will keep the name he had in the Resistance, Morin. Holed up with them and the vermin in the basement, there is also Vladimir Jankélévitch who tells the little five-year-old girl stories and who will later write: 'Forgiveness died in the death camps.'[23]

At the tender age when children's lips still bear the traces of mother's milk, Florence was wondering whether, if the

Germans tortured her, she would have the courage to keep silent, in spite of the pain. One day she and her mother are stopped by soldiers of the Gestapo. 'Your papers!' They are clearly forged. Just as he is about to arrest them, the German patrol commander decides in the end to let them go on their way.

'Das kleine Mädchen ist zu schön. Und wir werden sie nicht alle festnehmen können!'

'The little girl is just too pretty. And we'll never be able to arrest them all.'[24]

And then there are the rumours that fly around. Her father, André Malraux, has reportedly been killed. But he hasn't been, he is well and truly alive and, what's more, they meet up again on a bit of pavement at the Liberation. Both of them, the little girl and the hero, have braved death; they match each other in fearlessness, and the first thing he asks her – a marvellous question – is 'What book are you reading at the moment?'

The problem that René Julliard referred to at length during his conversation with Françoise is that she is a minor.

Of course, from a marketing aspect, that's terrific.

But from every other aspect, the fact of being a minor is a complication – all the more so when you're a girl. It is 1954, which means that a married woman, even if she has come of age, even if she is older than her husband, cannot be in charge of her own property, open a bank account or have an occupation without her spouse's permission.

René Julliard knows that the parents of young Françoise have not read the manuscript for he has made a point of asking her at their first meeting. Now the publisher is anxiously wondering whether, having read the book, they will agree to sign their daughter's contracts. If they were to refuse, there would be a three-year wait before the book could be published, during which time he would have to ensure that the little minx didn't find herself a husband.

'Will your parents agree to the book's being published?'

'Yes, yes,' replied Françoise casually, 'my parents are great people.'

So now Françoise had to inform them that her book would very soon be published.

And now they had to read it.

To know that hundreds, indeed thousands, of strangers are going to read your words is, depending on the individual writer, either vital, or energising, or theoretical, or problematic.

But to have your manuscript read by those close to you is an altogether different matter, and just as unwelcome as if they were to open your bathroom door while you were naked in the shower. All parties are embarrassed: we have to act as though none of it ever happened and must not speak of it except briefly, with an apologetic smile, and then we try not to think of it any more. I think this is almost always the case, since, in my view, anyone who writes a book that enchants their parents might well question the relevance of their work. (Yesterday I was at a book reading by an author I like who is as young as Sagan was, and he brought up the very topic as a joke when he said, 'My book is intended to be read by everyone except my mother.')

It must be assumed that Françoise was not entirely comfortable with the subject of her book, describing, as it did, a symbiotic and quasi-romantic relationship between a father and a girl who was not unlike her. When she arrived back at Boulevard Malesherbes after her three-hour meeting with René Julliard, the whole family was already seated at the table for the Sunday evening meal: her parents, her brother Jacques, her sister Suzanne and Suzanne's husband.

Suzanne and Jacques would have been severely punished if they had arrived back so late for dinner on a Sunday. But with Françoise it was different. It had always been different.

'Have you seen the time?' asks Marie Quoirez.

'I've found a publisher for my book!' exclaims Françoise, by way of excuse.

'Wonderful, but go and give your hair a quick comb and then come to the table.'[25]

It is Sunday again.

Two weeks have gone by. Marie, Françoise's mother, has invited some friends round for the afternoon. Françoise makes herself scarce – not for fear of being bored, since Marie and her friends are somewhat outrageous types. There is Marie Faucheran, who on one occasion had to be rolled up in a Persian carpet from the drawing room to prevent her shooting Pierre Quoirez dead with a revolver. There is also Odette, known as 'Lady Scott', one of the few women to have joined the parachute commandos during the Second World War. At least, so she says. And there is Claude Pompidou, who is not yet a president's wife but whose husband swears that, at the Quoirez establishment, you are dining 'at the best table in Paris'.[26]

Françoise knows that all her mother's friends are going to grill her about the forthcoming book and that is the last thing she wants. So she decides to take herself off in her father's Buick – she has suggested to Véronique that she will come and collect her and that they will go for a spin along the Seine.

In the days immediately following the meeting with René Julliard, the level of excitement had been high, the very air that Françoise breathed seemed different to her: she was going to be published. Everything around her, objects, times of day, passers-by, her parents … everything seemed to be part of a new universe – a universe in which *she was going to be published*.

But gradually the initial excitement had faded, just as the flavour of an infusion gets weaker the more water you add to the pot. And this was quite simply because the position in which she found herself felt, in fact, so right; it felt so normal that Françoise should be published, it wasn't some life-changing event, no, her life was simply going according to plan. So there you have it; ultimately that Sunday, 31 January, was like all the Sundays that had ever been and like all those that were still to come, no more, no less.

Her parents had read the book.

Marie had made no comment, other than to point out a few errors, expressing surprise that her daughter should want to be a writer and yet still have a poor grasp of French grammar and syntax.

Pierre had congratulated Françoise, merely remarking in his cheerful way, 'It's very good!'

That was all. There was nothing more to be said. Life went on as it always had done in the Quoirez family. What they really thought of the book, deep down, in their heart of hearts, is their business. And to tell the truth, my daughter is not yet old enough for me to be able to imagine how it must feel to read a book your child has written. It must be one of the most disturbing experiences a parent can have. Of course, I could always ask my own parents, two of whose daughters are writers. But I won't.

Driving through Paris, Françoise reflects that it is the last day for sending seasonal greetings, according to the rules of etiquette as prescribed by Gisèle d'Assailly, her publisher's wife. Françoise thinks of that advertisement for Perrier sparkling mineral water which 'wishes you health, wealth and happiness in 1954'. Just then Françoise realises that she is passing a bridge, the Pont des Arts, at the very spot where she made her vow on the morning of 1 January with Florence.

Further on, she sees staff in the windows of Galeries La Fayette dismantling the Christmas displays, which this year have been on the theme of Peter Pan. In front of Place de l'Opéra, an elderly nursemaid is pushing a navy-blue pram. To Françoise it looks like a little coffin mounted on wheels. She tries to banish that thought because, if she doesn't, the dead children who sometimes haunt her will come back.

The Seine has frozen over. Françoise has never seen such a thing and neither have her parents. The lock-keepers have the job of breaking up the ice to safeguard the working of the locks. Big lumps like icebergs come away and float off. Françoise, at the wheel of the Buick, watches the chestnut sellers – the scent of the chestnuts mingles with the charcoal and the smell of horse dung.

A lorry is parked in Rue Saint-Martin. It's loaded with worn canvas sacks. The delivery man wears a peaked cap, like a ticket collector's on a train. He is whistling Cora Vaucaire's 'La grosse dame chante' and he gives Françoise a nod. Smiling, he thinks to himself that you don't often see such a young girl at the wheel of a black Buick.

This is Paris in an era when cars park beneath the Eiffel Tower, there being as yet no underground parking areas nor any ring road. There's no Montparnasse Tower or Pompidou Centre either; instead there is a hosiery manufacturer's and a shop selling slippers. The city is like a huge building site, though Paris at night in 1954 is still spangled with stars and planets.

It is so cold that the market traders in Les Halles have lit a brazier on Place Sainte-Opportune to keep warm. It is so cold that at night the temperature is set to drop to minus fifteen degrees. It is so cold that an unknown individual called Abbé Pierre will broadcast the following appeal on Radio Luxembourg: 'My friends, we need your help! Last night at 3 a.m. a woman froze to death on the pavement of Boulevard Sébastopol, clutching the document that, two days ago, had authorised her eviction …'

In her car, Françoise is pondering.

At 3 p.m. she is due to speak to her publisher on the telephone.

They have both decided that it would be preferable for her to use a pseudonym. But she still hasn't come up with one. And the fact is that she'll have to do so quickly now, as the mock-ups of the book have got to be designed.

Françoise really likes the idea of having a pseudonym, firstly because almost all the writers she admires have one: Stendhal, George Sand, Gérard de Nerval, Guillaume Apollinaire and Paul Éluard, from whose work she took the title *Bonjour Tristesse*.

Bonjour tristesse.
Amour des corps aimables.
Puissance de l'amour
Dont l'amabilité surgit
Comme un monstre sans corps.

And, there again, taking another name is like getting married, not to a man, but to a woman, for that is what she feels she is doing in espousing the muse of literature. Far from being a disguise, this name to be worn like a made-to-measure garment fills her with a desire, not to become someone else, but to become fully herself.

She has been mulling it over for several days but she has still not the slightest idea.

By the time she gets back home, Françoise has only half an hour to think of a new name — it's always the same with her, she does everything at the last minute, once it has become urgent, when she's really up against it.

René Julliard has made it clear to her: the later the mock-up is started, the later the book can go into production and, as a consequence, the later it will be published. Now, that is something that Françoise certainly does not want: mid-March already seems to her to be light years away.

'I just can't think of a name,' sighs Françoise. Julia is making an *anguille* (a so-called 'eel'), a dessert typical of Cajarc, the pastry coiling round and round until it resembles a huge snail.

'Look in the directory,' she replies, without glancing up from her baking implements.

Of course! Why has she not thought of that before? Now, the directory with the sweetest names, the most beautiful, unexpected, enchanting names, whether of places or people, is Marcel Proust's *In Search of Lost Time*, whose parts Françoise has devoured in the wrong order of course, beginning with *Albertine Gone*. To have read Proust when she was fifteen, to have taken him to her heart, was to have embarked on an education in two spheres, life and literature – the latter of which has no rules.

In reading Proust, in discovering the magnificent obsession, the uncontrollable yet controlled passion that writing was, I also discovered that 'writing' was not an empty word, that to write was not an easy thing ... [27]

Minutes before the phone is due to ring, Françoise dives into the volumes of *In Search of Lost Time* and leafs through the thousands of pages, one after the other, turning them as feverishly as if they were the pages of a catalogue from which she was choosing her wedding dress.

The names flit past before her eyes, quiver on the lines, the

Vicomtesse de Vélude and the Princesse Sherbatoff, Madame de Varambon and the very loquacious Duc de Sidonia; there are also the Demoiselles d'Ambresac, so very wealthy, on holiday in Balbec with their parents; all these names are making her dizzy for, come what may, Françoise has to choose one of them. Yes, a name will come up as surely as a number on the roulette wheel in a casino – but, for the moment, the white ivory ball is spinning round the track.

The names that appeal to her, because of their strange sonorousness, are those of Mademoiselle de Stermaria and Zélia de Cambremer, the Princesse de Caprarola and the Prince d'Agrigente ... But the music of the name is not the only thing that counts, the character's role in the book has to be of significance, as in the obvious case of Bergotte, the writer, admired and envied, inspired and ailing, who keeps company with the Duchesse de Guermantes – before dropping dead in front of a painting by Vermeer.

Yes, Bergotte is a good idea, thinks Françoise, even if it sounds rather too feminine for her taste.

'Julia, what do you think of Françoise Bergotte?'

'Oh no, that sounds dreadful, it's like "idiot".'

So Françoise dives back into *In Search of Lost Time* and her gaze comes to rest on a sentence from *In the Shadow of Young Girls in Flower*:

Odette, Sagan qui vous dit bonjour.

It's not the word 'Sagan' that first catches her eye.

It's the word 'bonjour'.

Seeing it written there in Proust's book, in black and white, that simple word 'bonjour' that she has borrowed from Paul Éluard's poem, it is as if all those instances of 'bonjour' were joining hands and leaping from book to book to reach her, the little girl writer. 'Bonjour' forms a genealogical connection, a secret link between those great men and herself. So she reads the paragraph in its entirety.

'Odette, Sagan is bidding you good day,' observed Swann to his wife. And, in fact, the prince, turning his horse to face forward with a magnificent flourish, as if in a grand finale at the theatre, or circus, or in an old kind of tableau, was directing towards Odette a grandiose, theatrical salute ...

The Prince de Sagan, who had existed in real life, appeals to her because of all that is whimsical and ostentatious about him and because he is always dressed in the latest elegant style. Part dandy, part cavalry officer, 'in Paris he held sway over a crowd from fashionable society, as well as over people of a more dubious sort'.[28]

Françoise stores that name up in her head, then continues with her search, pausing over Borange – gosh, it would be funny to take the name of a grocer-cum-bookseller from Combray.

And while we're about it, why not Combray? 'Françoise Combray' has rather a nice ring to it, nicer than Françoise Borange. Françoise imagines how these names would look on her, just as, when faced with a rail of clothes, in your mind's eye you immediately picture the dresses superimposed on your body. So there's also Elstir, the painter and Odette's lover, with his sweet-sounding name. And why not Vinteuil? It's rather pretentious, rather obvious. There's also the Marquise de la Pommelière, nicknamed 'la Pomme', and Monsieur de Schlegel, who knows the language of flowers by heart.

Then Françoise's gaze alights on this sentence:

> It is true that those great men saw, at the Guermantes', the Princesse de Parme and the Princesse de Sagan (whom Françoise, hearing her always spoken of, and believing there to be a grammatical requirement for the feminine, ended up by calling 'la Sagante').[29]

The first thing that stops her in her tracks is the presence of her first name, 'Françoise', just as the presence of the word 'bonjour' had done a little while before. Françoise and Sagan are brought together in this way by the grammar of the Proustian sentence acting as a mirror that inverts the normal order of things. But here it's no longer a question of the prince, rather, of the princess.

Françoise is enraptured with this dual identity, half man, half woman. It encompasses both the decadent dandy and the grand society lady, who was received wherever she went as if mistress of all, encircled by princesses of her own rank and by the strings of pearls round her neck. The image that will cling to her legend is already contained in her name, for it is a name that says one may drive sports cars in bare feet with painted toenails, that one may lose at the casino and cadge money from the doorman to get home with, a name that says one will love both men and women, because what counts is the fact of loving – not wisely perhaps, but well. In choosing this name, she is choosing everything that is coming her way, that is approaching with giant steps, just as, in children's stories, the shadow of the ogre looms ever larger on the wall.

At that very moment the telephone rang. Françoise Quoirez had found her name. Henceforth and for ever she would be called Françoise Sagan. And seeing the words written on my page, I realise for the first time that Sagan is an anagram of *à sang* – it speaks of blood.

For ten days now I have not been living in my own flat at all.

My daughter is away on holiday and a friend who has gone abroad to work has lent me her little doll's house of a place in the Paris suburbs. The walls resonate with the sounds of the neighbours going about their lives as if we shared the same space, which I find pleasant and reassuring.

Leaving aside the phantom neighbours that I live with, I am beholden to no one, or virtually no one.

I am there only for Françoise.

I think of her constantly.

I speak just of her, constantly.

This very day I am struck when reading the following sentence of Sagan's: 'I saw a beach, with myself on the beach and a little boy beside me.' I believe that every young woman creates for herself an ideal photograph within her heart. This secret photograph of hers guides her every step. In the past, one image gave me courage whenever something hurt: 'one day I shall have a family' and in the photograph there were children, the father of the children – and me.

That particular photograph is no longer possible. It's existence turns out to have been fleeting. I must accept the situation. But I am not able to.

A memory comes back to me. When I was pregnant, we had wanted to call our daughter Françoise, but in the meantime Rebecca and Emmanuel had found a cat in Brittany and had brought her back to Paris and given her that name. So we abandoned the idea.

I am thinking back to those happy times. I am thinking back to 1 January 2010. We are waking up after spending the first night in our new flat and I am saying to myself: *All your life you must remember this day*. This first of January, when happiness has put its arms around you and placed on your lips a stinging kiss whose sweetness you must always remember.

Yes, all my life I shall think back to 1 January 2010. But I know today that, if that love did not endure, it is quite simply because there is no such thing as love.

… you are becoming cerebral and sad. That's just not you.[30]

So, following this advice from Françoise, one evening I accept an invitation to dinner.

Julien has heard the news; regarding our separation, he says that he is very sad for us; he appears to hope that things are sorting themselves out, and I believe they are.

He offers to take my mind off things.

I accept by asking him to take me to Brasserie Lipp, since, as I tell him, that would make me very happy; it's a place I like a lot. In reality it's because I am planning soon to write a scene set in that restaurant: I would like to write about Françoise and Florence going out for dinner together with the money Pierre Quoirez had given them in a roll of banknotes.

*

When I enter the restaurant, it is not my friend Julien but my characters I look for in the sea-green colour of the tiles with their motifs of exotic plants, beneath the dazzling chandeliers.

And I try to glimpse the faces of two little thirteen-year-old gamines – for that would be today's equivalent of the age they were then – dining together on their own among all those well-off, established people the same age as their grandparents. I am 'under the spell' of Françoise, as so many others have been before me. Nothing but her is of any interest to me, I am entirely under her influence. What's more, I am dressed this evening *à la* Peggy Roche, red dress, red tights, leather boots and red lipstick – the only things missing are the spectacles. You might say that I stride into this famous brasserie honking my horn.

In the end we don't talk about my separation at all, but about the book that Julien should be writing: for fifteen years he has been jotting down on scraps of paper, two inches by two inches, all the expressions that he wants to remember in life, snatches of conversations overheard, phrases that sound just right to him, passing thoughts of his.

He shows me photographs of his cellar: the floor is littered with hundreds of thousands of notes, which together seem to form a huge sea of foam.

'I've set about classifying them,' he tells me, before going on to say, 'Talking to you, one always has the feeling that a part of you isn't there.'

'Yes, I know. The father of my daughter used to accuse me of that all the time. He used to say that I didn't listen to him. It's true that, when he asked me a question, I often didn't reply. But I don't do it on purpose.'

'Is it because you're not interested?'

'No, it's because my mind is always on my books, all the time. I think that, initially, I appealed to him because I wrote. But later that began to be a hindrance – I mean, how it affects everyday life. It's always the same, you see. You leave people for the very reasons that attracted you to them in the first place.'

'Are you writing your next novel?'

'No, I'm writing a book on Françoise Sagan.'

There's always the same reaction to the words 'Françoise Sagan'. Julien's face lights up. He smiles. He repeats it: 'Ah, Françoise Sagan!' It never fails. It's like magic.

I tell him about the incident with the clairvoyant, which makes him laugh. We leave the brasserie and go to La Hune, the bookshop where I have ordered books that were published in 1953 and 1954.

The bookseller is very nice. We joke together and, since the books have not arrived, I ask him whether he can recommend something else instead. We get into conversation.

'Where are you from?' asks Julien.

The bookseller doesn't reply. He looks at Julien, expecting him to enlarge on his question.

'The way you speak, your unusual accent, what is it?' he insists. 'It's the same with her.' Julien points at me. 'Whenever she speaks, you know she comes from somewhere different. You can't place it exactly, but it's her own place, her own strange way of talking.'

'I speak very quickly, it's true,' admits the bookseller. 'I'll tell you something. In the past, on certain evenings, a small woman would come into the shop here. And because of the way her hair fell over her face, I recognised her immediately, not because of her face, which had changed a lot, but because of her hair. It was Françoise Sagan. She used to come to the shop to buy books. And whenever she found that it was me at the cash desk, we used to lay bets as to which one of us could talk faster. And we would begin to talk at top speed. It was so funny. We laughed a lot.'

Coming out of La Hune, I bellow at Julien, 'Aha, you see! I didn't lie to you about the clairvoyant! Why does the man in the shop start talking about Sagan just like that, out of the blue, without our having said anything? We were just talking about this and that, and he comes out with Françoise Sagan. You see! She's here, she's everywhere.'

For the first time in your life to see your name on the cover of a book – a cover you have so often dreamt of and imagined and that is suddenly there before your very eyes – it is not just a figment! I do not believe there is a single writer who, on seeing this, has not experienced strong, mixed feelings of aversion and fascination. For even though the cover is only an image, it is nonetheless an image that has all the potency of a deed. It is an image that says: 'The person who wrote this is now a writer.' Previously they were just writing, now they are a writer. They may be a good or a bad writer, that is not the issue. What does it matter? The cover of a first novel is a sacrament, the outward sign of a mysterious consecration having taken place, whereby the author now belongs to a community that he has dreamt of belonging to all his life, often since childhood.

Françoise Sagan calls in at Rue de l'Université to see the mock-up of the cover of her book, which is going into production soon. As she parks her father's Buick alongside René Julliard's Cadillac, Françoise is happy. She is now beginning to live her life, having for so long dreamt of doing so – and there is no more intense pleasure to be had than that.

The selfsame morning she has received a call from Éditions Plon. In fact Michel Déon, a reader for that publishing house and a journalist with *Paris Match*, thought her manuscript was terrific. But Charles Orengo, the managing director, had let three weeks go by before phoning the girl.[31]

I can imagine Françoise accepting the compliments, then listening politely to the advice.

'Of course ... a lot of things would need to be revised ... not just on the level of syntax, but also as regards the narrative structure of the book ... your writing is still very immature and unsure of itself ... that's only to be expected ... you'll learn quickly ... if you're willing to do so, we'll work on it together.'

I am certain she takes great pleasure in letting him talk on, before admitting to him that, regrettably, she has agreed a deal elsewhere.

When Françoise sees the mock-up of her cover with the name 'Françoise Sagan' on it, she smiles as she wonders: Who is this woman being credited with having written my book?

But before long, and to the end of her life, it will be on seeing the name 'Françoise Quoirez' that she will experience the 'strangest feeling of strangeness'.

Of course, she would probably have preferred the solemn, cream-coloured style of cover favoured by Gallimard, with its red and black borders and the three letters NRF (for *Nouvelle Revue Française*) that seem to float like a ship on the vastness of literature, in a fount that is both exacting and sure of itself and that makes no concessions. But fate has decreed otherwise and she is going to enter in by a different door, belonging to a more recent, more business-oriented and less literary firm. Sure, it's a lot less chic, that border in a pine-green that is only slightly fashionable, and the words 'Bonjour Tristesse' breaking out of the frame, as if determined to get through a window that is too small for them. The capital letters of the name JULLIARD seem to be a cheeky imitation of the capitals of GALLIMARD, like those counterfeited products that play on the resemblance between their name and the original in order to deceive the purchaser.

But so what? thinks Françoise.

So what?

She is proud of herself and she knows that her book will be read.

That's what matters today.

But it's not the only thing that matters.

What matters to her is to dash straight off to the Hôtel Rochester.

'By this evening, or by tomorrow at the latest, we need five thousand blankets, three hundred large ex-American Army tents and two hundred catalytic stoves. Bring them as soon as possible to the Hôtel Rochester, 92 Rue La Boétie.'

A baby of three months has died in the cold in Seine-Saint-Denis at the back of a disused bus where its parents spent the night. Then an old woman froze to death on the pavement of Boulevard Sébastopol. These two corpses are haunting Françoise, who wants to respond to the appeal by the *abbé* whom no one has ever heard of: she can at least bring pullovers and shoes that are mouldering in a cupboard in the Quoirez home.

'You'll have to wait for your mother's permission. She'll be back this evening,' says Julia.

'No, no, it can't wait. I have to go now. Do you want other children to die overnight?' retorts Françoise.

Julia Lafon has devoted herself to the Quoirez family for twenty-three years. She is a young woman from Cajarc, the village where Françoise was born in the ancestral home at number 45 Boulevard du Tour-de-Ville.

Cajarc and the limestone plateaux of the Lot are where it all began, an enchanting domain that must for ever remain inviolate,[32] the only place where Sagan will find a little peace. But this is not something Françoise knows today. She is still too close to her childhood to cherish it; on the contrary, she wants to get away from the place at any price, not spend her holidays there any more – nowadays she finds them deadly boring. She prefers the Côte d'Azur and the joys of Hossegor. But one day soon she will realise that that land of childhood is sacred and immutable, and that nothing can substitute for games played in abandoned houses with children of her own age or tramping through fields accompanied by pets and imaginary friends.

From the month of May, the meadows were already bowing under the weight of summer. The tall grass, limp from the heat, was leaning over, drying out and splitting right down to the earth. Further on, above the pond, hazy wisps of vapour trailed in the evening air. And the house itself, with its wrinkled pink façade – the house with its upstairs shutters closed on some secret and its downstairs French windows staring wide-eyed at some surprise – seemed like an old lady who had nodded off on the brink of succumbing to the pressure of uncertainties.[33]

*

Julia belongs to this magical land, which she left in 1931 to become cook and nanny in the Quoirez household. Her grandfather, Lucien Lafon, was a miller in one of the neighbouring villages. Julia was present at Françoise's birth and virtually raised her, reading her stories every evening, among them *Monsieur Seguin's Goat*, that tale about the nanny-goat, so strong and brave, who chooses death in exchange for a day of freedom. But at the end of the story Françoise didn't cry: she understood Monsieur Seguin's little nanny-goat very well.

'At last!' said the poor creature, who was simply waiting for daybreak before she died. And she lay down on the ground with her beautiful white coat all stained with blood.

Then the wolf leapt on the little goat and devoured her.

Balancing precariously on stools and piles of books, Julia and Françoise, the one as short as the other, get up on tiptoe to slide a rectangular box down from the top of the wardrobe. It's one of those big trunks, covered in treated black canvas and with brass studs, designed to fit on the back of cars. Françoise's eyes open wide, as if it were the sea-chest from *Treasure Island*.

But both women immediately catch their breath when they discover what is in the old trunk. Having lifted aside some pillowcases and inhaled the scent of dried-out lavender mixed with the smell of mothballs, they find a set of garments for a little child.

It is a baby's layette, carefully folded.

There is an ivory rattle and a cradle medallion.

There is a christening robe and a catalogue from the toyshop Au Nain Bleu.

And a silver christening cup engraved with the name Maurice.

Julia trembles from head to toe, for she knows that Françoise was never meant to see the contents of the trunk. No one has ever told her. No one has ever spoken to her of Maurice, the little boy, the baby, who died of dehydration in his cradle.

Around Françoise everything in the room begins to spin, as she sees Julia, who is fighting back tears at the sight of the baby clothes, shut the trunk hastily and clumsily.

For there are no real secrets in families. Secrets quietly bide their time before making themselves known. And while they patiently wait, they reveal their shapes in the silences.

Topics that are categorically avoided, a name that everyone stumbles over, stories that are referred to in a single brisk sentence ... all these conversational acrobatics result in a distorted perception of reality. The efforts of those close to us, our parents, our wife or husband, to make us blind to something that is actually there produce in our brains, through an association, not of ideas, but of silences, the outlines of a buried narrative that they are seeking to conceal. It's the same as in that optical illusion called Kanizsa's Triangle, where the brain produces the effect of contours that are purely subjective. In the 'empty' parts of the drawing, we perceive a triangular shape that is illusory but that we interpret and reconstitute in a way that renders it palpable and real. You can clearly see the triangle, even though it doesn't exist.

Thus Françoise was not surprised to discover a baby's layette hidden in the trunk in her parents' bedroom. In a sense, she had long been waiting for that moment; she had been waiting for them eventually to explain to her the reason for her night terrors and for those images that, at any moment of the day, would sometimes intrude upon her imagination. She had been waiting for the time when she would at last understand why dead children often came to haunt her and speak to her. Her discovery, instead of being painful, brought a sort of relief – how good it is to be able to put mute suffering into words, so that irrational fear may be turned into actual grief.

Then Julia told her about the birth of Maurice, what a happy little boy he was, always smiling, and about his sudden death. They had found him lifeless in his cradle – he had stopped breathing. There was a heatwave that day. Julia wasn't there. Who had found the child dead? Was it Marie or Suzanne? It was never very clear and no one had ever spoken of it again.

The weeks and months following the accident had been terrible for the whole family. The Quoirez couple, normally such merry, fun-loving people who loved to organise fancy-dress dinners and play tricks on the neighbours, had opened the door of their home to despair. Life had come to a standstill, until the day that Marie had felt her breasts hard and swollen and had experienced a strong craving to eat crab and drink white wine. Those signs had always been unmistakable as far as she was concerned: she was pregnant again. She had looked at her husband and had asked him to drive her to Deauville in his Graham-Paige Sharknose convertible to eat seafood. Pierre had understood what that meant; he smiled and there were tears in his eyes.

Marie had not envisaged having anything but another little boy, who would be in every particular like the child that had passed away, only more robust.

She had been so sure of it that she was astonished to hear her mother exclaim, 'It's a girl!' when the child was delivered, in the same room and even the same bed where she had given birth to her other three children. She turned the name she had chosen for her boy into its feminine equivalent and took the little girl in her arms. She was a tiny, sickly little thing; they would never be able to let this one out of their sight, and everybody loved her dearly, madly, excessively and they only had to approach the child for her, miraculously, to make them smile with happiness.

And so, from her birth, it was enough for her parents to look at her living and breathing to start laughing the laughter of those who have emptied themselves of all their tears.

Baby Françoise was allowed to do whatever she pleased. Everything was permitted. She was given every kind of gift.

I had to teach her to type on my Remington. She was the boss's daughter. The demands she made as a spoilt child annoyed me a bit. Seeing her at the wheel of her electric motor car or on her horse, you realised that she would always do things differently.[34]

Françoise and Julia stood for a long time side by side without saying a word. Françoise was thinking of that little boy who, in a way, had accompanied her throughout her childhood like a ghostly Siamese twin. He was with her when she drove her first toy car, when she fell off her bicycle, climbed trees, played with the sheep and ran through the fields.

Maurice had always been with her, since her birth.

The two women tidied the things away as they had been and put the trunk back in its place. They did so in silence. Then Françoise took from her closet two warm sweaters that her mother had bought her for Christmas, the astrakhan coat that Suzanne no longer wore because it was too tight round the waist since the birth of her daughter, and two silk scarves, one of them an Hermès which her father had given her for her fifteenth birthday, a big square of material, olive-green on an off-white background, depicting four carriages designed by Hugo Grygkar. It was immaculate, no holes or tear stains and no smell about it. She had taken from her wardrobe all that was most expensive and precious and she packed it all up in a big suitcase and went off in search of a taxi.

She said to the driver, 'Hôtel Rochester, please.'

'Well now,' he said, 'you're the third person I've taken there since the start of my shift. If it's still as chaotic as it was before,

I'll drop you at the corner of the Champs-Élysées.'

And indeed, when they got to where Rue La Boétie begins, Françoise was struck by the sight of the crowd milling around and swelling that narrow street, making it like a blood-bloated limb. Some folk were laden with parcels, while others had got rid of theirs and were trying to extricate themselves from the throng; there were cars stuck in a jam, hooting their horns, there were society women whose fur coats concealed Bar suits and swirly skirts, there were nuns in their immense white wimples that were like sheets of drawing paper blowing up into the sky, department store employees who had come to drop off blankets and clothes, housewives carrying piles of sheets and workmen bringing tinned food. All these people were queuing in the cold, in front of the revolving doors of the Hôtel Rochester, over which three flags still flew.

Suddenly Françoise hears a murmur run through the crowd, directed at a man with a beard. They are glimpsing for the first time that profile which, with its long, sparse, wispy beard, beret and pilgrim's cape, makes him instantly recognisable. It is Henri Groués who, during the Resistance, took the name Pierre, and who has been nicknamed 'Abbé' ever since he began trying to recreate in the Paris suburbs a utopia where the weakest are helped by their fellow men. Abbé Pierre cannot get over the throng of people who have been arriving since he launched his appeal around midday.

Very rapidly, in the hour that followed, nearly a dozen had turned up, then two dozen, and the two dozen had become hundreds; they thought it would stop at that, but in reality they were going to have to receive thousands of people and mountains of cardboard boxes in the hotel lobby, so many, in fact, that they would soon have to requisition the departure hall of the Gare d'Orsay to store it all.

Breaking away from the crowd, a man goes up to the *abbé* and hands him an envelope containing a million francs in notes of ten thousand. 'I'm ugly enough for you to recognise me again one day,'[35] he says.

But that's not all. A few days later the young *abbé* is to receive an invitation to go to the Hôtel de Crillon, that old luxury hotel that looks like an office block. There, Abbé Pierre will meet a little man who is world-famous but whom he himself doesn't know because he has never been to the cinema.

'I owed you millions. I'm not donating them, I'm giving them back. They belong to the tramp I used to be and whom I have come to personify. It's only right,' he will explain, handing him a cheque for two million francs. It is Charlie Chaplin.

When she gets back home late that afternoon, Françoise shuts herself in her room. She doesn't want to see her parents, or her brother or sister, all of whom are bound together by the life they had before she was born and by a secret they have been sharing for eighteen years. How could they have convinced her that they loved her more than anything, that she was their favourite child and adored sister, and have lied like that? Françoise is breathing the air of her new life and, to prove it, she lights up a Chesterfield – it's the first time she has smoked alone. The gestures involved are strange, almost unreal, but the smoke she exhales as she looks at herself in the mirror in her childhood bedroom is like theatrical fog, a prop that emphasises her new richer life and self. Françoise Quoirez observes the gestures Françoise Sagan makes as she smokes: she notes the femininity in the turn of the wrist and her manner of tilting her chin to bring the end of the filter to her lips, lowering her eyelids a little while doing so, just like those baby dolls with their plastic eyelashes which blink when you lay them down.

That is how Françoise appears in my imagination – for I have never read anywhere that she went to the Hôtel Rochester in response to Abbé Pierre's appeal. I have no evidence for it, but I cannot see how her generous heart could have done anything else or done it otherwise. As for the discovery concerning Maurice, I can only imagine how that too would have been, for she never referred to it in her books, still less in interviews, which she was adept at managing so that little was revealed.[36]

'Did she talk to you about her dead brother?'

'No, never,' replies Florence.

'But did you know about him?'

'No, I didn't. I found out when I read a biography of her.'

'I can understand that a family, especially of that era, might surround the death of a child with the deepest secrecy. But what I find strange, and what I cannot grasp, is that she, who always spoke so freely and had a love of truth, never shared that tragic story, not even with her closest friends.'

'You have to understand that it was indeed a different era. And then, it's Françoise we're dealing with.'

I have written nothing for ten days. I just can't progress. The springs are dry. Nothing flows from my fingers. It's like when you are playing at dice and the numbers that come up drive you to despair.

I was supposed to be writing a scene dated 15 February 1954 and set in the Café de Flore where, in a corner, while Françoise is getting tired of waiting for her book to appear, Boris Vian is writing a song, 'The Deserter'. Pierre Herbart would be sitting beside him. But I haven't the strength of mind for it, nor the inclination.

How am I to make up for these lost hours? I won't make up for them. Suddenly, and for the first time, I am struggling with this book. I am afraid that Françoise will abandon me if I don't work hard enough. I must take fresh heart and reconnect with her.

At 170 Boulevard de Magenta, among the neo-Egyptian columns of the Louxor cinema, its cobalt-blue mosaics interspersed with gold scarabs, cobras and heads of pharaohs, I see Françoise at a showing of *Si Versailles m'était Conté*. She is sitting uncomfortably in her Girl Guide-style skirt, a skirt that she will never ever wear again.

Sacha Guitry's latest film has just come out in cinemas and it's quite an event. Not only has there never been such an expensive film, but it has been shot at Versailles and it brings together all the best-known actors of the day, as well as a young starlet who plays Mademoiselle de Rosille, the mistress of Louis XV: Brigitte Bardot. Sacha Guitry wanted an actress who would 'not cost much' to play in a scene opposite Jean Marais. Brigitte is the same age as Françoise, just a few months older. Her face has appeared on the front cover of *Elle*. She is only eighteen but, already, her marriage to a Russian with an unpronounceable name has been reported in the papers – she too has had to ask her parents' permission.

Françoise Sagan looks at Brigitte Bardot's huge bust on the screen for, in truth, that's all you see when she appears in the film in her virginal white satin gown. Françoise thinks of her own breasts which are small, so very small. What must it feel like to have a big bust? That's an important question, a nagging question, that generations of girls will carry on asking.

I take pleasure in imagining the paths of these two girls crossing there: they have so much in common, being two girls from the bourgeoisie who will decide to enjoy the bodies that have been constructed for them, bodies schooled in classical dance, in riding and in the discipline that goes with wealthy neighbourhoods. Once launched on postwar French society, these two children will overturn all the rules, will fascinate men and seduce youth.

But on that day, 17 February 1954, they are not yet of any consequence, or barely so.

Brigitte Bardot is just another pin-up, whom Jean Gabin is shortly to refer to as 'that thing that walks around stark naked'. In the same vein, one day not too far off, the critic Étiemble will write of 'the twin evils of our time, Coca-Cola and Françoise Sagan'.[37] Both girls are promises of things to come, from the same background, a French bourgeoisie that is traditional yet given to whimsy. Their mothers are alike, being women who love to be surrounded by company, who love to dress well, wear big hats, drink champagne, spend their holidays in the mountains and forget about wartime restrictions as quickly as they possibly can.

Françoise and Brigitte are two distantly related cousins living in a France that is ready to pin a bad reputation on them, to reproach them for being what they are. They shall be called to account. For, whether they like it or not, the wheels of destiny have begun to turn. There is nothing they can do any more to stop them from turning. They will learn to their cost that it is never a good idea to be women by whom scandal comes.[38]

For the girls of their generation, Françoise Sagan and Brigitte Bardot blaze the trail to freedom and sexual emancipation, but they are also, conversely, a weapon to be turned against their own side. They are two children who are used in order to terrorise women, French women, the women of the Resistance, those lone women who have had to take risks, who have had to work, who have been arrested – some of them – and tortured, while others among them have had their heads shaved to pay the price for France's wrongdoing. Women, through force of circumstance, have become the foot-soldiers of everyday life and now it is really time for them to step back into line, to deal with children and household tasks. Those middle-aged women, their bodies worn out by pregnancies, who have had to assume power wherever there was a power vacuum, are today laying claim to their desires, not in the realm of sexuality, but in the realm of their own identity. An overwhelmingly masculine society is going to curb their aspirations by terrorising them with their own children, with girls who are incorrigible and free and whose bodies are unassailable.

I had lunch with Louis in the little Japanese restaurant on Rue Mazarine where he joins me, since I am working all day in the library of the Institute. He has grown a moustache for the part of Jacques de Bascher which he is to play in a film.

I say to myself: Louis is immersed in the sixties and I'm immersed in the fifties, each of us in our own way acting out the life of someone else. All of a sudden I look at Louis and I realise that, because of that one thing, because of my unhappiness in love, I have completely forgotten, rejected and discarded the Louis who, in 1954, was dear to the heart of Françoise.

At the time, Louis Neyton is her boyfriend. They write letters to each other because he is studying in Grenoble. He is one of her brother Jacques's friends and eleven years her senior.

The writer and biographer Jean-Claude Lamy, who was Françoise's great friend, is kind enough to come and see me to talk about her. He refers to the love affair at length.

'She liked tall men, the quite lanky sort.'

'What did she think when she read your biography of her?'

'She glanced through it, like this' – he pretends to be someone flicking through a book absent-mindedly – 'and then she said simply, "It's funny, it's as if it were the story of someone I don't really know."'

I must, of course, immerse myself in the account of that love affair. I ought to find the letters that she wrote to him dejectedly: 'I'm lonely, I'm far from you.' I ought to reinstate

Louis Neyton in my book. I believe that Françoise uses this idealised lover as a means of passing the time; wearing her jersey-wool dressing gown, she likes to nibble the croissants she has bought in Rue Jouffroy, all the while reflecting that she has a smitten lover somewhere who sends her love letters.[39] The Françoise of 1954 is no rebel: she dreams of having a family, a girl and a boy, and a husband. On the other hand, she likes to flirt, to have fun and to make love freely, before the time comes for stepping back into line. In short, she asserts the right to enjoy the same kind of youth as a boy, which, for a girl, is indecorous. You might even say scandalous.

What's more, today Françoise has a date with Louis, who has come to spend three days in Paris. But before they meet up, she must go to Bourdin the printer's, to be there for the production of her book. Now *there's* something to make her heart beat a bit faster. She knows that she will be bowled over when she sees her words typeset on the big Linotype machines in a noisy room filled with the acrid smell of ink, where dozens of women tap away on the keys of gigantic typewriters, just as in the scene from *The Man Who Loved Women* in which Charles Denner, noticing one of the typists wearing a blue dress, asks her, 'Is it still possible to change something?'

'Yes,' the young woman replies.

'Make the dress blue. I'd like it to be blue.'

All those words written one after another, those hundreds of thousands of letters typed one after another, are making her giddy. What if she never managed to write again? wonders Françoise. And what if it were the only book she succeeded in seeing through to the end? It's a question that all writers ask themselves: will they be able to start again? If not, it would be terrible, she's well aware of that, for she will never be able to do anything else in life and, anyway, it's all she has ever wanted to do since she could walk and hold a pen. She began by writing plays full of bloodied knights and captive queens that bored her mother to death, and then poems. Next, she wrote short stories, which she sent to the editor of *France-Soir*, but they were never accepted, never published. She also remembers that, when she was thirteen, one summer in Cajarc, she wrote a short novel that began with a dreadful car accident. She had called the heroine Lucile Saint-Léger, a name that she will later give to the heroine of *La Chamade*.

The novel opened with a car going into a skid. Lucile Saint-Léger was in it. The car overturned on her and the radio went on playing. And that's where it ended.[40]

Written when she was young, it was a novel full of premonitions. That's the problem with books, you must pay attention to what you put in them: they always catch up with you in the end. Don't ever nurture that secret dream of living a storybook life. Your dream might come true and then you would discover how tragic it is to become a character in a story.

This evening Françoise has a date with Louis Neyton. The young man rings the doorbell of the family apartment around 6.30 p.m., as decorum requires.

Pierre Quoirez opens the door.

'May I spirit your daughter away to dinner, Monsieur?'

'Offer accepted, on just one condition: that you NEVER bring her back!'[41]

And Louis Neyton understands the joke as he sees Françoise walk up, smiling and pulling on a pair of grey gloves that she will take off as soon as they get to Louis's hotel room near the Gare de Lyon, and Louis, my Louis, comes into my bed. We do not make love, we do not even exchange a kiss, but we talk together softly, calling each other by the ridiculous pet names of the past, my Louis, gentle as rainfall and better than anyone at making you laugh, and we fall asleep wrapped in the serenity of those far-off days and a youthful love affair.

At the kiosk in Avenue Marceau, Françoise has bought her mother the latest issue of *Le Nouveau Fémina*, which is just out.

The previous day, Pierre and Marie Quoirez had dinner with friends in Boulogne-Billancourt. When they arrived in the building where their hosts lived, they went to the wrong floor. Pierre entered the flat of the downstairs neighbours shouting, 'Here I come galloping, galloping, galloping in!' while pretending to be a rider on his horse. But when he got to the far end of the hallway and saw the bewildered faces of a couple in their pyjamas, he went back in the direction he had come from, shouting even more loudly, 'And off I go galloping, galloping, galloping out!'[42] There was laughter all round at this anecdote, the dinner was truly hilarious and the wine flowed. Naturally, Pierre and Marie's friends were curious to have news of the budding author: 'And when is Suzanne's book coming out?' 'Oh, no, it's Françoise who has written a book.' 'At her age? It can't be!' 'Have you read it? Does she mention you in it? Do you think she'll be awarded the Prix Goncourt?'

Looking back the next morning, Marie is vexed at having had to reply to the stupid, nosy questions of their acquaintances. If only she knew what lay in store for her!

For the moment, she has sent her daughter out into the cold of that first day of March to buy her magazine, prior to explaining to her that it might be better if she were to consider returning to classes at the Sorbonne. She can't keep just padding around in circles like a lion in a cage.

'You know, when your book comes out, you might have a few signing sessions in bookshops but, after that, you'll have to have something to occupy yourself with. What are you going to do between now and the holidays? I really can't stand having you under my feet all day long any more.'

'I'm going to write another book.'

'Write another book! But you could do both, study and write, like Simone de Beauvoir,' Marie says with a sigh, before starting to read an article entitled 'Mademoiselle Chanel is Back' that Jean Cocteau has written for *Le Nouveau Fémina*.

The doorbell rings. Yet Marie is not expecting anyone.

Françoise has forgotten to tell her parents. Her publisher's press office has sent over a photographer whose job it is to take the shots that are to be used in 'promoting' the book.

Standing at the door is a very small woman, her hair styled like a child whose mother has tried to flatten a too thick mop. Beneath her raincoat she wears a black suit with sloping shoulders, and she has a a Rolleiflex slung across her chest.

Sabine Weiss is thirty but looks ten years younger. She doesn't look much, yet she is one of the most gifted photographers of her generation.

Françoise was not at all expecting to see a wayward schoolgirl turn up in the guise of a photographer – they could easily be the same age, and this young woman is doing a man's job, which both mother and daughter are impressed by.

'Have you been a photographer for long?'

'I have always taken photographs of things. My father taught me when I was a child. Would you mind if we went and had a look together at the different places where we could set ourselves up?'

'Of course not. I thought we could go into the study.'

'Yes, if you like.'

'Did you always want to be a photographer?'

'I bought my first camera with my pocket money when I was twelve.'

'Shall I sit here, like this, at the typewriter?'

'Yes, that's good. There's natural light. Just act as if I wasn't here.'

'You must be joking. I couldn't! You *are* here.'

'Wait, that won't do. I don't know why, but it looks ridiculous. Is this where you wrote your book?'

'No, it's my father's study.'

'So where did you write your book then?'

'Oh … in lots of places … in cafés to start with, a lot of it in bed … and also lying on the floor.'

'We'll try that. Here, show me. Lie down just like when you were writing your book.'

'So, like this.'

'You see, all I have to do is to come across an authentic situation for the camera to tell me it's just right and I can take the photograph.'

I have spent a long time, a very long time, looking at that photograph of Françoise Sagan. I have studied the whiteness of her wrist, the bone that sticks out like a lump, her delicate hands, like those of a Botticelli Virgin, her boyish hairstyle whose rather rumpled state indicates the offhandedness of the girl – she has not even given it 'a quick comb' – and her sensuous, jaded pose, accentuated by one of those velvet cushions on which newborn babies get photographed.

It is a touching photograph. Françoise appears particularly pretty in it. (I have read several times that she was not 'photogenic' and that pictures of her do not do justice to the grace and charm that radiated from her face.) It's a photograph taken before the unleashing of the storm, before the madness that was to come. When I see pictures of today's writers, I wonder why I find them to have less 'depth' and be less enigmatic than those of earlier writers who have so captured my imagination.

Browsing Sabine Weiss's website, I discover that one can send her an email.

I write her the following message:

Hello.

I am a writer currently working on a book about Françoise Sagan and the year 1954.

You photographed her for the publication of her book *Bonjour Tristesse*. I would like to talk to you about that.

Thank you,

Anne Berest

I am hoping that she will get back to me soon. Anyway, today I received two other replies.

Florence Malraux phoned to say that she liked the first few pages of my book and that she would encourage me to go on with it.

And Julien, to whom I had given the opening section of my manuscript, sends the following text message:

It's good. Carry on with it. Except for the scene where René Julliard reads the manuscript. It's pure kitsch, like something out of Labiche.

He is right, I am going to have to look at that part again, but not straight away. This evening I have decided to 'live like a boy'.

I make a few phone calls, to this person and that, to find out the whereabouts of any parties in town, what's on offer, just as in the past when we used to go out every night and Paris belonged to us.

The shape of the evening quickly emerges: drinks in a studio behind the Cité Universitaire, followed by a party at the house of an American actor in the eighth *arrondissement*, all ending up, no doubt, in a fashionable nightclub. It is such a long time since I have done that kind of thing and I think back to the words of the clairvoyant: 'may your drinking make her tipsy … Let yourself go … Let her enjoy some final moments through you.'

In the crowd I notice the colour of his hair first of all. I glimpse him in a corner of the kitchen at the American actor's; the actor himself isn't there and probably doesn't know that his impressive town house near Avenue Foch has been taken over by about a hundred people.

It is the colour of a child's hair, so blond that it is almost white, with a blondness that is redolent of holidays by the sea, of August, of sun mingled with salt; it's a blondness that children lose as their childhood morphs into adolescence and then, with adulthood, it is no more.

For a long time I find it hard to look at him properly because the whiteness of his skin, accentuated by the black of his beauty spots, like small, shiny insects that have landed on his face, disturbs me.

I am disconcerted.

Because I have never, never before experienced what is coursing through my body at this moment. It is what a man may experience when he comes face to face with a girl, that powerful sensation of being in thrall to a face; you are on your knees, you have lost the battle and you know it.

'Shall we go back to my place?'

Yes, yes. How could I say no? I do believe it is Françoise replying for me, and we find ourselves in a taxi, Françoise, the young man and I. I assess the situation: he must be almost ten years younger than me. Obviously it has never bothered me when it has been the other way round, but this time I want to sink into the recesses of the back seat, melt into the upholstery, vanish into the green glow of the traffic lights. We get to his place. I am not so much walking as creeping along behind that soft, pale colouring of his, which is offset by the powerfulness of his man's body. I am aware already that I will never tire of looking at these things. I have never known anything like it in my life. I have lost all sense of myself, as if overwhelmed by a picture or a landscape.

It's a student bedsit that I crawl into, with course documents spread over the floor, earplugs, scribbled post-it notes on the wall, books scattered here and there. We are drunk; I tell him that I am planning to cut my hair to rid myself of a few bad memories along with it. 'Let's go for it,' he replies, seizing a pair of kitchen scissors, and all at once six inches of my long tresses, last cut when I was a teenager, fall, while day breaks and a ray of sunlight creeps over the carpet to what has been scalped, Red Indian style, and suddenly seems to catch fire. And I leave; we won't have exchanged kisses this morning. I set off in search of a Métro station. Lost in Rue de Lisbonne, I travel south, towards the Mediterranean, towards the very special green of umbrella pines. I'm broke, I haven't a bean. I look at the façades of the buildings, the green plants on the balconies. I am surprised at how light my skull feels; my fingers seek the vanished tresses. I realise that I do not even have the boy's telephone number, nor his surname – and I stop short in front of the blue street-name sign and I smile as I think of Françoise, for here I am at the corner of Boulevard Malesherbes; she would be delighted to see me in this dishevelled condition, so I push her gently away from me. *Françoise, don't start getting me up to all sorts of things; let's go back to 1954 when you were still only a more or less good little girl and not yet a model of offhandedness – I'm not ready for that.*

So we both go back to that first day of March, to the exact time, that terrible moment, when the first American hydrogen bomb explodes in the Pacific over Bikini Atoll.

How will she get through those days of waiting? She knows what to do at night. It's always easy to fill the nights. But it's different during the day; everyone is busy with their own activities – Florence is in her office at Gallimard, Véronique is at lectures at the university and her brother Jacques has gone back to work in London.

So Françoise goes for walks around Paris, since she still has ten long days to wait until her book appears in the shops and something happens at last.

She walks along the paths in the Luxembourg Gardens, where the chairs sit all alone in the cold, so thin that they look like bones, like skeletons of chairs. Going up Rue Soufflot towards the Panthéon, she meets a man delivering Valstar beers – 'bottled and pasteurised' – at the Kentucky Club.

Françoise loves walking in Paris and watching the knife-sharpener and the porters transporting calves' heads go past, watching men working on the roofs and black Citroën Tractions leaving the factory.

She is used to dawdling like this: at the age of twelve she was expelled from the Louise-de-Bettignies School, but she did not tell Pierre and Marie. She kept the disgrace of her expulsion secret – instead she happened to be a little poorly and they dosed her with vegetable broth and an infusion of thyme, and applied a camphor liniment.

For three months, from April until the school holidays, the little twelve-year-old Françoise set off in the morning with her satchel on her back. But instead of turning into the school courtyard, she went off at a tangent. For three months a little girl gave her parents to believe that she was going to school. But the truth was that she was walking around Paris until it was evening. Of Sagan's entire life, with all its outrageousness, I think that what surprises me most, and what I most admire, is this: that a little girl of twelve could spend entire weeks roaming around Paris without her parents realising and without being afraid herself.

It is more incredible than the millions of books sold, the fortunes spent, the carry-ons in casinos, the passionate love affairs: that small girl is my heroine. How I love little girls – they delight me, they fascinate me, I envy them for still being like boys, without curves or bleeding, yet with all the strength that women have. I do believe that there is nothing more potent, more monstrously potent, than a little girl of twelve.

Six years on, and Françoise Quoirez is still a vagabond, a bluffer and a free spirit, in a state of transition, not quite Sagan, but those are the same feet on the same pavements; the shadow she casts has barely changed; her breasts are scarcely discernible and her hips have not grown much wider.

Françoise draws up a wish list: one day she will earn so much money from her books that she will put banknotes in a hatbox for her friends to be able to help themselves without having the embarrassment of asking her.

She hopes that one day the President of the Republic will come and have lunch with her in secret, to gain a little respite from the crushing obligations of power. They will talk literature and share society gossip.

She dreams that one day she will be paid to write columns about New York and Venice. She will spend evenings in smoke-filled restaurants talking to men who, like her, will be writing books.

She will meet the writers she admires, Jean-Paul Sartre, Carson McCullers and even Tennessee Williams, and they will become not just admired elders, but true friends. She will move into a hotel so that she can drink cocktails and not have to make her bed.

One day she will earn enough money never to have to think about money again.

She dreams of a life as flamboyant as Colette's: Colette who danced naked except for a panther skin, who drove men and women mad, whose companions were princesses and very young men with the same taste on their lips, the red taste of delirious love, luscious as a cherry, who went to Saint-Tropez, that sunny little port that no one knew, and spent happy days there on holiday; Colette who did not take herself seriously and whom nobody, therefore, took seriously; Colette the ghostwriter, robbed by her husband, Colette-Zelda; Colette displaying her white breasts in photographs, magnificent breasts as soft as children; Colette whose name was 'Sidonie-Gabrielle' which, if you listen carefully, has within it the music of 'Sagan'.

Rereading *Gigi*, I am struck by the following description of Gilberte, which seems to me to describe, word for word, Françoise's appearance in 1954: 'She looked like an archer, or an unyielding angel, or a boy in skirts; she rarely looked like a girl.'

At last it's a day when something happens, for Françoise and also for me.

Her books have arrived at the press office in Rue de l'Université.

A postcard has arrived at my door as if by magic, with a few words from the young man.

I spend a long time looking at the card. I have placed it on my sofa near the window and I wonder what it is doing in my home. I can't reply to it, nor do I even want to. Better quite simply to act as if none of it had happened: the night without sleep, the postcard.

I am going to get back to work. I am going to get back to writing. I am going to reconnect with Françoise. I envisage her arriving late at her publisher's; René Julliard had been expecting her much earlier in the course of the morning. She doesn't realise how long it takes to sign books and write the dedications as required by the press office.

On the desk, piles of books are set out in rows, one behind the other – it's highly impressive. They have round them a red promotional wrapper bearing the words 'Devil in the Heart', in reference to the book by Raymond Radiguet which, ten years previously, had been a huge success.

No one has asked her opinion of the wrapper. Françoise is not sure that she likes it very much, for she knows only too well what it means. Of course, she understands that they want the media to highlight her age but she can already predict the consequences of such a legacy: the sarcasm, the false comparisons, the readers who will be annoyed by the analogy. At the very worst, the comparison won't hold up and at best she will be called 'a Radiguet in petticoats'.

But there is nothing she can say or do about it. The process of letting go is under way. The book does not belong to her any more, she barely still belongs to herself.

She has been practising her new signature, 'Françoise Sagan'. The Françoise bit is easy enough to write, but Sagan looks different every time – it'll come.

René Julliard explains in detail the ins and outs of signing books, for you don't address a journalist from *La Dépêche* in the same way as you would François Mauriac of *Le Figaro* or the members of the Académie Française as a whole. Françoise rolls her eyes: could she not write the same thing to everyone? It would be much simpler. At this point, René Julliard starts to laugh and agrees that she can write 'avec toute ma sympathie' to all. It is a dedication she will continue to use until her trip to America, where, after a whole day spent writing 'with all my sympathy' for readers who react with either amusement or discomfiture, she finally has it explained to her that 'in English it means "with my deepest condolences"'.[43]

When, with a numb hand and heavy wrist, Françoise escapes to breathe the cold air of the outside world, night has descended over Paris. But, in truth, she has put her heart and soul into the task, for example in her dedication to Colette: 'To Madame Colette, with the prayer that this book will give her one hundredth of the pleasure that hers have given me. Respectfully, Françoise Sagan.'[44]

Suddenly she is struck by the thought of all those books that are going to wend their way through the streets and arrive in people's letter boxes, at concierges' lodges, on Parisian doormats. There's no going back: in a few hours the first readers will be opening the book by a young unknown called Françoise Sagan and will be deciding, after just the first few lines or pages, whether to carry on reading – or not.

There is nothing for it but to light a cigarette (it has become a habit now, smoking alone), cross the road, walk a little distance to call in to see 'Flo' in her office at Gallimard and ask her to come and have a beer (not a shandy). Opposite the front door of the prestigious publishing house a woman has dropped off to sleep in a car. Françoise recognises her by her red lipstick and her Buddha-like eyelids. Françoise had so liked the sense of torpor in the woman's latest book, the noxiously torrid heat of *The Little Horses of Tarquinia*, and she ought to have been daring enough to tell her so, but Queen Marguerite, asleep, presents the radiant face of a drowned maiden whom one would not dare disturb.

'Love does not take holidays,' he said, 'that just does not happen. You have got to live out your love entirely, with its tedium and everything else. There can be no holiday from that.'[45]

Whenever Françoise meets Florence, she knows that something is bound to happen, because her friend is like a heroine in a novel: events will always come rushing to throw themselves at her feet.

Sitting in the lobby of Gallimard while the young woman receptionist goes off down the corridors to look for Florence, Françoise smiles. Just a few months ago they were two schoolgirls in scratchy skirts, yet today one of them works for Gallimard and the other is waiting for her book to come out. Gradually, like a drum roll getting louder, she becomes aware of her heart beating beneath her dress and is surprised to find strange thoughts occurring to her. She is suddenly aware that a certain destiny awaits her, a destiny that will be both cruel and exciting. She 'sees' the whole of her life to come, just as in the past, on one miraculous day, she saw the book that she was to write.[46]

Françoise thinks back to Florence's eighteenth birthday some months before. That day, her father, André Malraux, had summoned her to say, 'Get it into your head that the boys who will hang around you will be doing so in order to gain access to me.'

And the girl, with her soft curves and bright open face, had replied to him quite simply, 'Perhaps it will also be because I'm quite attractive.'[47]

There is so much that is effortlessly attractive about her that individuals, both men and women, are affected by her and charmed by her, without being able to explain exactly why.

'I think I liked listening to people,' Florence tells me, 'even when they weren't saying anything. Michel Leiris would often come to my windowless little office at Gallimard. He would sit down opposite me without a word and could stay like that for an hour, or two hours. To my mind he was just looking for a bit of peace. I was impressed by him. I had loved *Manhood*. I got on especially well with Jean Genet. Sometimes, when I arrived back after the lunch break, I would find a little note from him on my table: "When can you call by so that we can have a bit of a laugh?" It was an era of fantastic, unexpected encounters and Françoise loved to come and see me at the office. When she became famous through her book, Gaston Gallimard would always say to me, "Right, do what you can to bring her over to me" … but they had missed the boat.'

Yes, Françoise loves hanging about at Gallimard, and all her life will love the distinctive atmosphere in publishing houses. Now here comes Florence, smiling at her friend who has been waiting for her patiently, her head slightly tilted to one side, as usual.

'So, how was it at the press office?' she asks.

'My wrist is knackered. I think I've signed two hundred tons' worth of books. But it would be churlish to complain.'

Florence laughingly puts her two lovely little hands up to Françoise's ear and whispers, 'We're invited to dinner at Dionys and Marguerite's. I said I was bringing a friend.'

Their cheeks glow rosy from that feeling, so joyful and childish, that signals the beginning of one's golden age, that all-too-brief period between childhood and adulthood. Having waited for a long time in the wings, you are at last stepping out onto the stage of your life.

The girls arrive at number 5 Rue Saint-Benoît around 8 p.m. Marguerite Duras had moved into that street, with the Café de Flore on the corner as its magnificent portal, in 1943. She lived there with her first husband, Robert Antelme, then with the father of her son, Dionys Mascolo, but the three of them spend most of their time together, lunching on the terrace of Le Petit Saint-Benoît, a restaurant which is still there in its folksy decor of red-and-white check – it's not clear whether this is just a relic of bygone days or whether it has been done up to look picturesque. Françoise and Florence have bought a bottle of red wine there and are excited by the idea of spending an evening with writers from the Gallimard stable. Florence knows that she'll be seeing Edgar Morin, her wartime friend, but they will also meet the writers Raymond Queneau, Georges Bataille, Italo Calvino or, even, Francis Ponge and Maurice Blanchot, for Marguerite and Dionys have taken the words of Friedrich Hölderlin as their household motto: 'The life of the mind shared with friends and the thoughts that arise through exchanges both written and spoken are necessary to those who seek.'[48]

It's 'the Rue Saint-Benoît gang' as, later, people will say 'the Sagan gang'. The latter will not have a quotation as its emblem, nor any literary – still less political – aim. But in my view a gang is a gang, and gangs always come together for the same reason: to fight a common enemy, be it capitalism or boredom.

Marguerite Duras's apartment is nothing like any of the adults' apartments that Françoise is used to visiting. It is a kind of physical representation of the writer's thought: entering it is as if you were entering her memory. There are the two pairs of scissors hanging from a nail on the wall, fully opened, because open scissors allow you to find things that have been lost. There are newspapers, lots of them, books, objects acquired here and there and carefully conserved, for each one of them represents a world, and who cares whether or not they 'go together'? There are photographs stuck on the mirror above the mantelpiece, unframed, lipsticks and bottles of perfume, the imposing typewriter, strange pictures, coloured textiles, cushions faded by the sun, a wickerwork lamp, wooden toys belonging to Outa, the red notebook with recipes in it called 'The Lorry Notebook'; and the aroma of coffee beans roasted in the frying pan envelops all these objects in a warm nimbus.

'Ah, here are the girls!' cries Marguerite, as she emerges from the kitchen in her apron and an ivory bracelet.

'It smells very good,' says Florence politely, before introducing the girl who is with her. 'My friend Françoise … Sagan,' she says hesitantly – she still isn't used to it.

Marguerite orders the girls to make themselves at home. She senses that they are intimidated and when others are intimidated that in turn intimidates her. So, to distract from the embarrassment, she launches into a description of the Vietnamese omelette she has prepared for this evening. It's true there were good steaks at the market, but she didn't know how many people there would be in the end.

'And then, with steaks, one always comes to grief, as with tragedy, though the degrees involved are different,'[49] she laughs.

Françoise and Florence are the first women to arrive, whereas the men are already there. Françoise knows – she doesn't know how she knows, she just knows, that's all – that Marguerite Duras likes men. All those men in the life of a woman writer, the idea greatly appeals to her: big, strong men, men who relish the challenges life throws up, darkly romantic men, men who have their own cars (and Marguerite likes that too, a 'nice set of wheels') so if that is what it is to be a woman writer, to be loved like Colette and Marguerite Duras, then it's worth sacrificing everything for, she thinks, it's worth working for – even though, later, she is going to say the very opposite.

Françoise is not listening to the political discussions going on round the table: there is fury over the war in Indochina, which is rumbling on; in the newspapers the setting up of the camp at Dien Bien Phu is being hailed as a victory, yet Marguerite knows that each day brings with it new losses among the French paratroops. To Françoise, as to most French people, Hanoi is a faraway place on a map. Right now she is fascinated and thrilled by the spectacle of these creatures who dare to live a different kind of life. Monique Régnier has just arrived, so the foursome from *The Little Horses of Tarquinia* is now complete: Robert Antelme, his new wife Monique and even Outa, the 'child' in the book, who is playing on the drawing-room floor. This evening there is something about Marguerite, Monique, Dionys and Robert that makes them akin to Françoise's future characters, and even though the expression does not yet exist, you could say of them that, in their own way, they are 'Saganesque'.

Naturally, Marguerite is curious about the girl who is her guest and quizzes her.

'Françoise is bringing out a book! Next week,' adds Florence.

Round the table, people's conversations come to a sudden halt. The apprentice novelist is so intriguing that they look her up and down – will she be subjected to their teasing, or false deference, or astonishment? The worst would be to meet with indifference.

'Who's the publisher?' It's a killer question and one that, in Paris, they ask in order to trap you, because it means 'What are you worth?'

'Julliard.'

Naturally, for 'the Rue Saint-Benoît gang', it's the wrong answer. Julliard is such a jumped-up newcomer. Curiosity wanes. Even though Florence adds, 'Plon wanted her, but she had already signed ...' it is too late; they have congratulated the girl stiffly and moved on to another topic.

But the girl who, this evening, at the far end of the table, squirms on the edge of her chair out of shyness, who is pleased to be in that company, even if she is not 'of that company', will tomorrow, perhaps, be fêted throughout the world. Who knows? No one knows. In any case, none of the guests at the dinner can foresee it, for all their brilliance.

A few days away from the publication of *Bonjour Tristesse*, Françoise Sagan is merely an apprentice writer, somewhat looked down on by those who are her fellows for that evening. But soon she will be much more famous than any of the people round the table.

When Marguerite recognises the teenager's face in the papers, she will say to herself, 'So it was her, the girl who came to dinner.' And she will be surprised. And she will smile to herself for having forgotten that the unexpected always happens and that life is more improbable than fiction. And Marguerite too will sell several million copies of a book. In exactly thirty years from now. She has thirty years still to live before she will experience that particular frenzy. For Françoise it is now. Everything is in flux. All the time. The cause of my grief is also the reason for my hope: everything is in flux, all the time.

Things change. I must never forget that.

*

After my interview with Florence, I buy *Manhood* by Michel Leiris, which I have never ever read. I am staggered. How could I have studied literature for so many years and spent so much time talking about books and decided to become a writer without anyone making me read that work? Well, here's the explanation (for sometimes false questions elicit the truth): I had to wait until I was thirty-four and was at a precise point in my life to discover a book that begins like this: 'To cut a long story short, I have just turned thirty-four, I am of average height and I am afraid of losing my hair.'

It's the powerful self-portrait of an 'average' man who wants to be a writer. I close the book and grab my coat. I have arranged to meet my mother outside the crèche.

And then, on my way to the crèche, something comes back to me.

'Maman, I've just read *Manhood* by Michel Leiris.'

'Oh, right.'

'Have you read it?'

'No.'

'It's fantastic.'

'Oh, right.'

'No, really … fan-tas-tic.'

'I'm sure.'

'I'll lend it to you if you want.'

'Right.'

'Maman … one day when I was small you explained to me that, at the end of the war, Mamie had arranged for you to have a Catholic baptism because she feared for you as a Jewish girl.'

'Did I tell you that?'

'Yes, I remember it perfectly.'

'I see.'

'And you even told me that the man who posed as your godfather was Michel Leiris. Do you not remember?'

'It wasn't Michel Leiris, it was Pierre Leyris, a translator. Right, shall we go in?'

'OK, let's go in.'

And we go into the crèche.

The fifteenth of March 1954 is the day that Françoise Sagan's book *Bonjour Tristesse* is published. In the history of publishing and the history of literature it ranks as a 'historic' date.

But what happened that day in the life of Françoise Sagan? Not much, probably. She no doubt went to Julliard's in order to feel surrounded by people involved in the book's publication. She discovered how very lonely it is for a writer on such a banal yet such a special day.

The staff in publishing houses, who know the drill by heart, are able to gently reassure those authors troubled by the lack of ceremony. Françoise took refuge in the office of Rolande Prétat, in the sales division, to share a cigarette and a little emotion. Rolande is so gentle, with her plunging necklines and reassuring breasts, her Jean Patou perfume …

'… It's called Adieu Sagesse and I think of you every morning now when I put it on,' she says, smiling.

'I hope that will bring me luck!' replies Françoise.

'Of course. It's going to do very well. I've had very good feedback from the marketing people.'

'Really?'

'Yes, yes, really. Shall we bet on it? I've never lost out yet with my forecasts,' says Rolande.

'Great. Well … let's say that, beyond 100,000 copies, I'll give you a franc for every book sold.'

'Right, you're on,' cries the sales director in a burst of laughter.

It wasn't going to happen, for even though Rolande believed in the book, success in her eyes meant sales of 15,000 or 20,000 copies. However, she did not put Françoise right: authors, be they young or old – in this respect their age is immaterial – have no idea about the reality of sales figures … You might as well let them dream.

But everything is in flux. All the time. And in December 1955 Rolande Prétat will receive a splendid Christmas present from Françoise Sagan: a cheque for 100,000 francs.[50]

Françoise will not always keep her accounts but she will always keep her promises. Better to die poor than dishonoured.

On the front cover of the British magazine *Picture Post*, Brigitte Bardot is posing in a flowing red satin dress which might have been stolen from her great-aunt's wardrobe. She challenges us with her mighty tits and eyebrows, while the magazine's headline reads: 'Brigitte Bardot, two pages in colour'.

On that day, you will find no mention of Françoise Sagan in the latest issue of *Paris Match*. Yet Michel Déon, who had read the manuscript for Plon, has suggested her as a subject.

The response was merely 'No, no, she's not well enough known.'

As for Rolande Prétat, she has just replaced the receiver after a long conversation with her brother Jean, who goes round bookshops as a sales rep.

'The book is taking off in the most amazing way,' he has warned her. 'The shops will have run out of copies by the end of the week.'

'Just fancy that! And there was no publicity.'

'You've got to do a reprint immediately.'

'I can't possibly. I'm on my own here until next week.'

And, in fact, Rolande's bosses, René Julliard and Pierre Javet, have both gone off to enjoy some winter sports. There is obviously no way of getting in touch with them and Rolande on her own is not permitted to take as important a decision as authorising a reprint. Not only does her position not give her the authority ... but as a woman she would run the enormous risk of being seen as an incompetent female issuing crazy orders in the absence of the company's men.

What should she do? René Julliard had decided on a first print run of 4,500 copies, a lot for a first novel, the average run of which is 1,500 – it has got to be said that everyone in the firm had been won over by young Françoise's book, sensing that they had a winner on their hands.

Rolande doesn't know what to do. Not to reprint would be a mistake: if booksellers ran out of books, they might lose a quarter of possible sales (the reader borrows the book from his neighbour or decides meanwhile to buy a thriller ...). But to issue such an order while her superiors are away is unthinkable. Why has no one foreseen such a situation?

While Rolande Prétat, with trembling hand, takes the initiative and orders a new print run of 3,000 copies, Françoise, completely unaware of the cogs that are turning in order to get her book reprinted, is browsing among the shelves in a bookshop.

For all young writers, the physical relationship with bookshops in the early days of the publication of their book is a delicate matter. (I myself always experience a kind of fear, I might even say terror, which lasts for some time and almost makes me cross to the other side of the street when a bookshop comes into view.)

Françoise, for her part, her curiosity getting the better of her, decides to go into a bookshop with the intention of passing herself off as just another customer. As she opens the door she hears the doorbell tinkling, but the peal of little bells is not followed by the usual 'Good day to you' ... The man seated behind the cash register is so absorbed in what he is reading that he has forgotten he has a job to do as a bookseller. At this very point he is completely wrapped up in Cécile, the heroine of the book that he is just getting into, and is enjoying a moment of illicit pleasure in which the girl's description of physical love (she being devoid of all morality in matters of the heart) is giving him such a large bulge in the trouser department that he is in any case incapable of standing up to greet the new customer.

I discovered the pleasure to be had from kissing. I am not able to put a specific boy's name to these memories – whether it was Jean or Hubert or Jacques, which are names familiar to all nice young girls.

The presence of an insubstantial shape moving about in his field of vision dismays him. The bookseller closes the book and hides it in the drawer below his cash register.

'What can I do for you, Mademoiselle?' he asks the girl. He is as shaken as a child whose parents have just caught him out.

'I'm looking for a book … one that has just come out … *Bonjour Tristesse.*'

'I'm sorry, but we haven't a single copy left.'

'Oh. Will you be getting any more?'

'I suggest you go elsewhere. We wish to preserve the moral tone of our establishment so we are not selling that book any more.'

But Françoise, who has recognised her book among all the others (by its thickness, by the colour of its paper, by the texture of its cover), knows full well that this man possesses one last copy which he refuses to sell to her. 'Thank you,' she replies politely as she leaves the shop.

I recall that the first big impression literature made on me while I was reading a novel was an erotic impression.

A book had the power to give me 'the hots'. I was twelve when I read *The Lover* by Marguerite Duras. There was no question of my being allowed to see the film at the cinema but on the other hand the book was easily accessible in one of my parents' bookcases. So that was what literature was all about – making extraordinary discoveries which one couldn't refer to out loud but which it was accepted could resonate silently in one's head, like those words which I read and reread and read again, hoping that all at once I would understand what they meant:

> I asked him to do it over and over, to do that thing to me. He had done so. He had done so through the lubricity that the blood provided. I could have died from the pleasure of it.

I was twelve and for me literature meant sex. There you are. It couldn't be simpler. I am one of those people that got their first pornographic thrills from words. I tell myself today that in fact I am not far removed from a girl of 1954, enjoying clandestine pleasure beneath the sheets with a book by Françoise Sagan – I have known the same thrill as those girls born forty years before me. Literature will never again, for the children of the future, be a gateway to the fabulous world of eroticism. I am not sad for those children, since, after all, the important thing for each person is to discover his or her own path to sexual enjoyment. But I am rather sad, it is true, for literature, since literature is being deprived of a fine role – it is rather like those ageing actresses in the theatre who know that they will never again be able to utter on stage the words of Molière's young heroine: 'Pussy has just had it.'

In the end I arranged to meet the student; his being so young puts a spring in my step and brings out an enterprising side to my nature – just as, in a new relationship, we have a tendency to invert the roles that characterised the previous one and make the other person go through the ordeals that we ourselves have endured in the past.

I have invited him to spend a day in Deauville, for it struck me as being impossible to end this book without at least once in my life experiencing what a casino is like. Françoise is attempting to feel, through my fingers, the smooth warmth of a gambling chip and deep down I am grateful to her for providing me with a novelist's pretext, though in actual fact the trip has only one aim: that of finding myself in a hotel room with the young man.

We have arranged to meet on the platform of the Gare Saint-Lazare ten minutes before the train leaves. I should have guessed that he would not be early, unlike me. The train's departure is announced. My heart becomes one big bruise at the thought of being left standing. But all of a sudden his blond head appears in the crowd; he's walking along calmly with a strange bundle over his shoulder: 'I put my things in a pillow slip because my suitcase is at my parents' house.'

We take our seats on the train and talk about the colour of his hair. He tells me that in Japan, in restaurants, men would come up to touch it, for they had never seen anything like it. I say, 'It's true your hair is a wonderful colour,' then he opens

Le Canard Enchaîné, before leaning against the window and closing his eyes as if I were not there. I am relieved that he is going to sleep because it saves me from having to think up new topics of conversation and I can take advantage of this momentary respite to finish the book I am reading, a biography of Maurice Ravel by Jean Echenoz.

Having read all the biographies of Françoise Sagan, those of some of her contemporaries, and certain novels that came out at the same time as hers, as well as books about Paris in the fifties, I now have to read biographies written by writers. For the same reasons that books have taught me how to live, authors have taught me how to write, and in Echenoz's book I find answers, ways forward and solutions to the problems I am currently faced with. I am sure that Françoise Sagan would have liked this book, which tells of the musician's final ten years, because Echenoz has a painter's eye ('The sea is so green it is almost black') but also because of his skill in describing machines, especially cars.

When we arrive in Deauville, the blond opens his eyes and I close my book, somewhat put out by my reading, for if great books fire you up by showing you that anything is possible provided you are unconstrained and sincere, they can also force you to confront your own limitations. You think that you will never manage to write your own book.

Our hotel room is entirely decked out in *toile de Jouy,* with its comely swains and shepherdesses: the wallpaper matches the curtains which match the bedspread, not to mention the cushions. It's as if all that comeliness is urging us to 'Come! Come! Come!' and it almost hurts your eyes if you look too long at the walls.

We are as embarrassed as young newlyweds on the first evening of their honeymoon. You just can't avoid the bed, which takes up the whole room. However, we manage to act as if everything were perfectly normal by checking that we have our identity cards for getting into the casino.

I put on a dress when I get out of the shower; our belongings are all mixed up on the bed, our gestures are gradually becoming more relaxed and flowing and I am experiencing that excitement mingled with childish joy which I have not known for several months.

Once we get to the gaming room – not the room with the one-armed bandits, but where the 'tables' are – I have to exchange my money for chips. I settle down to blackjack, for roulette still makes a big impression on me and I daren't sit down at that. What is truly exciting in this place is the ceremonial aspect, the rules. Everyone is where they should be and plays their role as required. I can hear the sound of hundreds of roulette chips tumbling and each time it is as if something is shattering. The young man shows me how to play and straight away we have a win. Intoxicated by the champagne and by our success, we walk back in the direction of our pretty room with its *toile de Jouy*. Beginner's luck, they say. Walking through the empty streets of Deauville by night, after the day spent in his company, I wonder how this boy can be so detached from his own beauty, as if he were unaware of its existence. How can he be so indifferent to his own sharp – almost violently-so – qualities.

At around seven o'clock in the morning I slide noiselessly out of the bed that has become our bed. I can't sleep, and it's because of that skin, which is different in texture from the skin I have slept up against for years.

I am going to take a walk in the hotel, hoping to find an echo of Françoise's footsteps somewhere here. I am in that state of bliss that follows when you have conquered love.

It's Sunday morning and no one is awake, apart from a man near the conservatory, whom I catch sight of from behind and who is drinking coffee and looking out at the garden. He is wearing a suit jacket in grey wool and his shirt collar is up, but just on one side. He is sitting quite still and appears to be absorbed in whatever it is he can see. I bend down to get a glimpse of what exactly might be happening outside, but there is nothing, nothing at all. I go round the breakfast buffet to get a rather better view of his face, or at least his profile. I am impelled by that curiosity I have about people in restaurants who take lunch or dinner alone – for that is one of my own most prized luxuries, being alone and able to listen in to the conversations going on nearby.

I recognise him immediately. The incongruousness of the situation gives me licence to go and speak to him, the fact that he should be sitting there alone in this place. And that I should be up, and alone too, at the same time as him. It is all very strange.

'May I join you to drink my coffee? I know, it's very early, but we don't have to talk …'

'Please do.'

'That's very kind of you. When I get back to Paris I shall be able to say that I had breakfast with you in Deauville.'

'What are you doing here, and so early?'

'I am trying to cure my depression,' I say, laughing.

'You don't seem at all depressed.'

'I am, I assure you, terribly so. I am in the middle of a divorce. But meeting you has cheered me up. It's a great pleasure for me.'

'Thank you.'

'And what are you doing here, and so early?'

'I'm on the jury of a film festival.'

'I see. Do you enjoy that?'

'Yes. It makes a change. It gets me out of my rut.'

'Are you writing anything at the moment?'

'Yes, I am.'

'A new biography?'

'Err … no, not exactly.'

'When I was little, there was a copy of *Cherokee* on my parents' bookshelf and I don't know why, but the cover fascinated me, and the title, and your name – all those vowels surrounded by unusual consonants. But I'm sorry, I said I wouldn't talk and I'm rambling on. Anyway, I'm going back upstairs to bed. Apologies for having disturbed you but, although I can't explain why – it would take too long – meeting you this morning has been very special for me. It's like a sign, you see, a sign of encouragement that gives me the strength to do all the things I still have to do.'

And Jean Echenoz bids me goodbye, with a lock of hair falling over his large forehead and those washed-out blue eyes that have known all epochs. I am going back to Paris having, for the first time in my life, gambled in a casino, having for the first time spent a night with a man other than the father of my daughter and having met Jean Echenoz.

And it is all thanks to Françoise. I haven't forgotten my young friend from 1954. I continue to look at the calendar of that year, and write my book, while hers, every day, sells a few more copies.

Jacques Chardonne, a writer of the so-called 'Hussard' group, who was not exactly well-disposed to young women, nor indeed to the human race, wrote the following letter to Roger Nimier:

This week I read Françoise Sagan's novel. That girl comes from a good family, the family of great writers. There's no mistaking it, it's as plain as the colour of a person's eyes and the texture of their skin. It makes one's heart jump for joy. Talent is a unique thing; it has to be excellent in every particular, radiant, sharp and unblemished. One either loves the talent or is indifferent to it. If you love it, you do so boundlessly. And love like that arises from the exercise of rigorous judgement.[51]

More than 8,000 copies of *Bonjour Tristesse* have been sold by this date.

Dien Bien Phu has fallen.

The red flag with the gold star has been planted in the French camp – it is the beginning of the end for the colonial empire.

For Françoise, too, it's the beginning of the end, that is, if you accept the dictum of Madame de Staël: 'Glory is the dazzling funeral of happiness.'

Françoise is in something of a fix: an American, who does not exactly appeal to her but who does not leave her totally cold either, has offered to take her to Senlis, in the Oise, near the Forest of Chantilly. He is a poet and his friends are organising a *Bal nègre* like there used to be in the bar of the same name before the war, at 33 Rue Blomet, in the fifteenth *arrondissement*. Everything will be organised as it used to be by their sassy elders, with 'ti-punch cocktails, orgiastic dances and a few notes of the beguine to evoke the West Indies. Dancing, laughing and drinking: the very thought is enough to thrill Françoise. But, most thrilling of all, the American is to take her to Senlis on a motorbike, a Honda JC Benly with a 125-horsepower, four-stroke engine, based on the engine of the Dream, seldom seen in France – and what's more, he dresses like Marlon Brando, the actor in the recently released film that everyone is talking about, in a white T-shirt and a Perfecto leather jacket, which to her mind is both ridiculous and exciting.

Françoise very nearly got to drive the Honda, like in *The Wild Ones*; there were only two votes in it. But at six o'clock precisely she received a phone call from her publisher telling her to put on an evening dress, a string of pearls and her mother's gloves, and be ready for the party that would be held that evening in her honour. She was the lucky winner of the Prix des Critiques. Françoise was, of course, delighted for her publisher, who set such great store by prizes, and she was flattered to have been selected for a distinction with so much prestige attached. But she heaved a sigh: so that was what success meant, a long series of obligations.

The jury for the Prix des Critiques is made up of sixteen men, one of whom is a woman – and even she has a man's name – who are going to join hands and form a circle, with the girl in the middle, and then whirl round her in a dance that no one will ever be able to stop. Let us break into that circle to be a little part of it. Let us too join hands with them to discover who these gentlemen are who are frivolous enough to award the crown to a little girl, which they do, perhaps, in a spirit of challenge or provocation. Whatever the truth of the matter, these are not men who were born yesterday, no, they were formed in the First World War; these are men who have seen other men die, who have fought on the field of battle; some have been in the Resistance; they are men who have held the dead in their arms. Émile Henriot served in the dragoon regiment during the Great War; a journalist, a man of letters and a writer, it is he who coined the expression 'Nouveau Roman'. He is now sixty-five. Gabriel Marcel is exactly the same age and, similarly, has a moustache, though his is a flowing white moustache that looks like a huge silkworm. Henri Clouard was born the same year as them, and is an admirer of Maurras and a Balzac specialist. Marcel Arland, a winner of the Prix Goncourt and a mere fifty-five years old, had opposed the Surrealists and is co-director of *La Nouvelle Revue Française* along with Jean Paulhan, just exactly sixty years old, a prominent member of the Resistance and a friend of Sartre's; his writings on literature are still invaluable reference works for students of French. Jean Blanzat is not yet fifty; a figure in the Resistance, he has obtained the Prix Femina and the Grand Prix de l'Académie Française. Jean Grenier was the philosophy teacher of Albert Camus, who dedicated his first book to him. Robert Kanters is director of the science-fiction section at Denoël and, most notably, is to introduce Philip K. Dick to a French readership. Robert Kemp, seventy-five years old, is a literary critic and later a member of the Académie Française. Thierry Maulnier, theatre critic for *Combat* and *La Revue de Paris*, played a part in the setting-up of the review associated with La Table Ronde and will also be elected to the Académie. Armand Hoog is a literary critic whose first novel was awarded the Prix Sainte-Beuve. Maurice Nadeau was orphaned in the Great War, was a prominent member of the Resistance and is uncompromising as a publisher and unsurpassed when it comes to recognising talent. Roger Caillois, who will in his turn become a member of the Académie, is a sociologist and literary critic and had been a friend of Paul Éluard's. And then there is Dominique Aury, the token woman, who is about to publish, in June, perhaps one of the greatest works of pornography ever, *Story of O* written as a love letter to her lover Jean Paulhan. And then there are Georges Bataille and Maurice Blanchot, the two writers of immense stature on the jury, who each in his own way is defined by transgression.

If I attach importance to this rather long, perhaps rather tedious list, it is because we have to understand just what the prize represents in the France of 1954: it is an award which, given the jury's prestige, commands respect, guarantees the admiration of readers, but also makes a big impression on those in 'the trade'. It is a famous prize, which, after the war, was bestowed on Albert Camus for *The Plague*, a prize that has come to be noted, evaluated and discussed, a prize in the hands of the 'experts' in literature, since the critics, whom it represents, are credited with having the gift of perceiving the 'objective' merits of a particular literary talent.

What is it that they have acclaimed in this young girl's work? The classical form embodying a contemporary mindset, the freshness of expression, the choice allusions, the elegant concision, the fluency of the dialogue … but all that is not enough. It has to be a book that spoke of them and of their generation. In it, a child is observing how these old gentlemen live and she pronounces them to be admirable: 'I much preferred my father's friends, men of forty, who spoke to me with courtesy and affection, and treated me with the consideration of a father or lover.' Ah yes, youth is a beautiful thing; after all, young people are not children any more, so one is permitted to go to bed with them.

In Sagan's later novels, the different generations, far from being in conflict, will enjoy mixing, living and making love together. In that respect she seems most unlike the young of 1968: she wants to live with her father, just the two of them, whereas, in future, children will want to make a clean sweep of the patriarchs. And yet, and yet, she plays more of a role than you might think in that coming revolution.

Françoise Sagan, five foot four and seven stone, arrives late at the party given in her honour, for there has had to be a very frank discussion with René Julliard as to the possibility of reconciling professional obligations with going to the ball in Senlis.

The photographers, the journalists, the petits fours: everything is in place including the 100,000 francs in cash presented to her by the sponsor of the prize, Florence J. Gould – previous winners had received a cheque, but it has to be said that they had come of age and were thus in possession of a bank account.

Marie Quoirez, who is to find the rolls of banknotes in the tea-towel drawer, will wonder for a moment whether she isn't seeing things,[52] while Pierre will give this advice to his daughter: 'At your age, money is something you have to force yourself to spend.'[53]

How is she to quell the terror that success brings? Answer:

with alcohol. Françoise drinks whisky and doesn't say a lot, but fortunately the guests round the table have much to talk about among themselves. All those adults. For they are adults! They play games, they give rewards, they distribute good and bad marks. But how can they desire or hate to the extent that they do?

'What makes you write?' I write to be rich and famous, she says, kicking the question into touch. For would it not be ridiculous to tell the truth: that one writes to give voice to the poem, to move people, perhaps to change them, to transform them through words, to make contact with the soul ... Doesn't such talk make you want to die of boredom? It's much more fun, and much more respectful of literature, not to take yourself seriously. But that's how the myth of her offhandedness gets started. At the end of the day, it is probably the only thing that she *will* take seriously and will work at without let-up, just as, by dint of hard work, the principal ballerina eliminates all trace of effort from dancing. Putting all one's effort into feigning the absence of effort is like painting white on white: it's not a colour that's easy to see.

To take her mind off the motorbike trip that she has just missed, Françoise thinks of the second-hand Jaguar XK120 that she will be collecting from the garage next week. She would like to set off south in it directly on leaving the garage. She would go with her brother Jacques. They would head for Cannes or Nice or perhaps even Saint-Tropez, which she has never been to. She would spend all her money, for, after all, this shower of banknotes will soon dry up and, when eventually she becomes her parents' young daughter again, she will certainly have to work hard and write a book – a good book, a great book, she tells herself. It will be a book to be proud of, as thick as a dictionary. And while Françoise, when she shuts her eyelids, is seeing red and green spots from the flashlights of the journalists, she tells herself that she should urgently begin writing the next novel.

But the problem is that the money is not going to dry up. Quite the contrary. Up to today she has sold 8,500 copies of her book. But a year from now, after the media scandal that the awarding of the prize is going to provoke, she will have sold 850,000 copies. Then it will be a million.

The next day, on the front page of *Le Figaro*, François Mauriac writes that famous article of his which will give rise to innumerable debates, so much so that the press cuttings for *Bonjour Tristesse*, when they put them on the scales, will weigh nearly two stone.[54]

François Mauriac, the Christian believer, who has but recently been the recipient of the Nobel Prize for Literature, sums up Sagan in the formulation that has since become famous: the 'charming little monster'. She will reply by saying that she is neither little, nor charming, nor a monster.

And so it was that the prize was given and the book was acclaimed, booed, hated, adored and read in secret; and thus it became necessary to sign new contracts, write articles for women's magazines, travel to Venice and go on a hectic tour of the United States, talk for months, years, decades, about a book that was written in six weeks, adapt it for the cinema, go from party to party, from jazz club to nightclub, drink litres of alcohol, pretend to be drunk in order to escape people, narrowly escape death as well, have her skull split open and her pelvis shattered, meet Bernard Frank never to leave him, form hectic relationships, drive sports cars barefoot, park her Jaguar behind the kitchens of Hôtel de la Ponche in Saint-Tropez, own a Gordini Type 24S, a Jaguar E-Type convertible, a Maserati Mistral, a Lotus Super Seven S1, as well as a Ferrari California cabriolet, win and lose fortunes in casinos, buy a house in Normandy early on the morning of the eighth day of the eighth month of the year, having bet on the number eight in roulette at eight o'clock that morning, buy a house simply in order to avoid having to pack up and go, buy a house in order to to be able to sleep peacefully in it after a night without sleep, buy a racehorse for the sheer excitement of it, love various men, have her wedding splashed on the front pages of the papers, be the target of a plastic bomb attack for having denounced the use of torture in Algeria, sign the manifesto of the '343 Sluts', be friends with Jean-Paul Sartre and François Mitterrand, surrender her lips to Ava Gardner and Massimo Gargia, laugh with Yves Saint Laurent and Pierre Bergé, meet Mikhail Gorbachev and Tennessee Williams, be obliged to justify everything she has previously done, explain herself over and over, be the recorder of her every act, be always brief and precise, say 'to make love' at the start of her life for it to be thought scandalous, say 'to make love' at the end of her life for it to be thought quaint, say 'to make love' and do so all her life, write other books, write plays, write lists of things to do that she doesn't want to do, write love letters and letters breaking things off, no longer have time to write at all, so much time does she spend talking about what she has written, no longer remember what she has written, the words she has thought up, the titles of the books she has published, never stop writing, until the end.

There will be all of that, but, unlike Flaubert's Frédéric and Deslauriers, when Françoise sums up for her friends – her women friends – the lives they have had, she will comment that they haven't made such a mess of things, she and they. And the reason for that? Perhaps it's because they will never stop furthering their 'sentimental education' so, in that respect, they will all their lives remain the girls they were in 1954.

I would like 21 June that year, Midsummer Day and her birthday, to be the day that Françoise sets off in secret in her new car as a fitting celebration of having reached the age of nineteen. Seated in her Jaguar, she is level with the ground; she can feel the speed through her body. The RN7 is narrow and dangerous – the motorway to the South has not yet been built. She drives her fine car as if it were a fine beast that had a mind of its own and would not always react instantaneously.[55] This would be the first time, I imagine, that she had gone to Saint-Tropez and this is how I would like to finish the book, on a note of sun and speed.

I got out of bed, I opened the shutters, and the sea and the sky thrust in my face that same blueness, that same rose colour, that same happiness.[56]

I myself have never been to Saint-Tropez. I decide to spend a couple of days there in a final push to finish the book. A friend suggests I could rent his aunt's studio. I would like to hear the echo of Françoise's laughter, her joy at being read and fêted, in spite of the frenzy that is starting up around her.

I quickly pack my case, with a yellow dress, a blue swimsuit and books for the train, including *La Chamade* – I really loved Alain Cavalier's film of it, without even knowing that it was an adaptation of one of Sagan's novels.

This 'writer's retreat' of mine is almost like heading south for a holiday. Before going to the station, I give my daughter Brigitte Bardot's song which we like to dance to: 'Tu veux ou tu veux pas?' and I kiss her on both cheeks – they are like brioches with specks of white sugar and I am going to miss them over the next two days and two nights.

Obviously I should have gone by car but I haven't driven since the day I took my test. So I opt for the train.

In my brightly coloured carriage, I read the description of Sagan by Tennessee Williams who, in 1954, wrote *Cat on a Hot Tin Roof* for Broadway.

Françoise Sagan met him the following year in the course of her great American tour, more colossal than that of any rock star. Watching through the window of my high-speed train as the landscape rushes past, I dream of Tennessee Williams, forty-four years old, Françoise Sagan, nineteen, and Carson

McCullers, thirty-eight, spending two weeks together at Key West, fishing, smoking and drinking neat gin. Françoise Sagan is later to write that those were two baking-hot, tumultuous weeks. In the description that he gives of her, Tennessee Williams speaks first of the terror that takes hold of him whenever he witnesses a young writer being lionised by the press.

> In the morning she was sun-bathing and swimming, and in the afternoon we went deep-sea fishing and in the evening, when it came again, she took the wheel of my sports car and drove it so fast, with such a gay smile, that I had to warn her of the highway patrolmen. I think a passion for speed is a healthy sign in a young artist: it shows that they know already the need to keep distance between them and the pack.[57]

Gradually, outside, the landscape is changing, the sky is becoming brighter, the sea is getting nearer and, on the spur of the moment, I send a message to the young man asking him to come and join me in the South.

Then I go back to thinking about the encounter between Matthieu Galey and Françoise. It took place, if I am to believe his *Journal*, on 3 June 1954, that's to say, a week after the awarding of the Prix des Critiques.

They arrange to meet in Les Deux Magots. Matthieu Galey gets there early and the question he asks himself while waiting for her is 'Will she disappoint me?' Then he goes up to another girl by mistake, just like Fabrice Luchini, the character in the film *La Discrète*. I try to imagine Matthieu Galey at the age of nineteen, right in the middle of his work on a study of Raymond Radiguet, which he is never to publish, even assuming he ever finished it. No matter: out of it came his encounters with Cocteau, Brancusi and Joseph Kessel, as well as his extraordinary *Journal*, in which he describes Françoise as follows:

> She is small and brown-haired, with round, sombre eyes, and barely looks as old as her eighteen years. No powder, no lipstick, her hair all over the place, her forehead hidden by a fringe. A brittle voice, talks fast; her speech is almost indecipherable, just the opposite of what she actually says, which is so fresh and clear.

Unusually for him, Matthieu Galey reckons the girl is very intelligent and their conversation focuses principally on questions of literature and love. She tells him that she once loved a stupid boy who was not interested in her and that she now blushes at the thought of it. She confesses that, for her, love is the only thing that is worthwhile and she would be prepared to give up all literary ambition for it. She claims that the ballyhoo surrounding her book has bored her stiff and made her punch-drunk. Matthieu Galey goes away from their interview quite charmed, and happy to answer the question he had put to himself: 'All in all, she has not disappointed me'. Many will think of Françoise as a promise that will not be kept, but has she ever disappointed anyone? I don't think so. And, anyway, there seems to me to be huge merit in being true, not so much to your actual promises, as to the spirit of what you promise.

Arriving in Saint-Tropez, I do of course find it difficult, in today's town, to uncover traces of the year 1954.

I search for "'the mad, mad sea that on the beach shatters its goblets of champagne", as Cocteau puts it, and that, here more than elsewhere, is frothy, unanticipated and refreshing. Then there is the countryside, real countryside nestled behind Saint-Tropez, and green, unlike the rest of the Maures Massif ...'[58]

I search for the little streets that Françoise loved so much and that she describes as squabbling among themselves; I search for the countless hours in which she loved to lose herself; I search for the paths beyond Pampelonne; I search for the houses basking in the sun and reminding her of large cats; I search for the sea that gradually takes on an authentically blue colour below the cemetery that poor Michel Tardieu skirts in *And God Created Woman*.

Walking on the beach, I try to visualise Françoise Sagan and Brigitte Bardot, meeting for the first time in the summer of 1955. Brigitte, with her head slightly bent, is making circles in the sand with her toe, as if she were pushing round an invisible shell.

They became, both of them, the most famous girls in France. And both were to come back from the brink of death before the age of twenty-five, Françoise in a car accident, Brigitte in a suicide attempt. Both will know what a lunatic thing fame is, and its laxness and decadence. It would require an exceptional character to stand up to what is going to be their lot: a life of satiety.

'Of course the youth of today possesses incredible nerve, a shamelessness that looks very much like genius or, at least, has no scruples about sending bursts of intelligence shooting out in all directions. Plenty of genius. Too much genius. A machine gun loaded with genius. What these young writers need on top of that is a bit of talent ...'[59] writes Cocteau that year.

Coming back to my rented studio, I get a message from the young man, who won't be joining me in Saint-Tropez. I am sad at that, so, instead of writing the last pages of the book, I compose this letter:

You don't want to come south to join me because, you say, you can't 'afford the train ticket'.

But at the same time you won't let me buy it for you, and your refusal saddens me.

Yet I do understand you. At your age I would never have agreed to an older man paying for a ticket for me to meet him. I would have thought: He takes me for a whore. Or, rather, I would have thought: Someone, somewhere, might say I'm a whore. I would have done a lot of thinking, instead of quite simply enjoying the trip and – why not? – enjoying my ressemblance to a whore.

I understand you, because not so long ago I was your age. I'm barely out of my twenties, and I lived through them without understanding anything. During that decade, which seemed very long to me, I missed out on everything and most of all I missed out on myself. I did not seize the opportunities that came my way; I did not take risks; I was afraid of dying before I had even lived; I was afraid of not becoming somebody; I was 'boxed in' by ideas of my own making and by a false idea of myself. For, yes, I had a precise and lofty idea of how the elements of my life had to fall into place, in a way that would allow me at last to come into my own.

You can't possibly imagine.

I went through my twenties without ever being unaware of myself. I wore my identity as if it were full of fragile promise, like a garment that is so new you don't want it to get shabby or stained, you only want to take it out on special occasions and in the end you never wear it.

I was waiting for my life to begin because I wanted it to just happen to me.

But today if you asked me, 'Would you like to relive your twenties, but differently?' I would reply, 'No.' For it is because I stopped myself doing so much that today I dare ask you to take a train. It's because I believed in the existence of fate that today I no longer even know the meaning of that word. It's because I was afraid of so much that today I am afraid of nothing. So I don't hold it against you for not taking that train. But just be clear that no one will ever give you back those two days that we will not be spending together.

Right now, at the precise second that I am writing these words, I would like once more to see the expression on your face that appeared the moment I told you that we mustn't see each other any more.

You asked me then if I had always wanted to become a writer. I didn't answer, because your question took me by surprise. So here, somewhat belatedly, is the answer I would have given you if you had come to join me here.

Yes, I have always wanted to write, long before I knew what it really means to write, rather as a child dreams of becoming a fireman, for the sake of the red uniform and the shiny fire engine. And then, one day, when the child is an adult, he is confronted by a fire and he realises that he has never thought about the fear involved, only the prestige, but that he is now going to have to put out the fire and, to do so, he is going to have to withstand the heat and the anxiety and the smell of burnt flesh.

I wanted to write in order to live the life of a writer, which seemed to me the only kind of life worth living, and I tried as best I could to make my life the story – whereas writing is the very opposite of that.

Writing means putting your life on hold for days, weeks, even months on end. It means believing that those who share your time are stealing it from you and wasting it needlessly. Writing means gradually cutting back on the story of your own life.

My other problem was that I had a very lofty idea of

what I had to write in order to become a 'writer', such a lofty idea that I didn't manage to write anything. I wanted to write a great book or nothing at all.

But one day – I remember it very clearly; I was the same age as you are today – I said to myself: You will never be Sagan. You will never write *Bonjour Tristesse* at seventeen, it's much too late for you. But you will write 'your' books. They will be what they will be and each one will be better than the one before. Or not. No matter. They will be the only thing that truly belongs to you, the only thing that no one will be able to take away from you. You will tell people stories and, if it keeps them entertained, they will be grateful to you. For it's no bad thing to entertain people. Wait till you get on a bit before wanting to instruct them or dazzle them. And while you may not yet be an artist, do not disparage the idea of becoming skilled in your craft.

That day, thanks to Françoise Sagan, I wrote the first page of my first novel, then the second page. And over the next two years, without stopping, I wrote all the subsequent pages. And I wrote one book, then another and yet another today. With every page I hear my heart beating out: So, that way of life is possible.

Today, with Françoise Sagan's help, I am trying to change the way I live a little by following her advice, all of which ultimately carries the same message: seek what *is* important, don't seek to *be* important.

That is why I am able to write to you today and tell you

how I loved exploring that chamber we shaped out of the night that was ours. In a day's time, or after a thousand nights, spent with one woman or a thousand, suddenly you will remember me.

As for me, I shall never forget our kisses or your face, or your fearfulness or mine.

A.

The next day I walk alone through the streets of Saint-Tropez and on the beach. On the terrace of Sénéquier I breakfast on marmalade and pain de mie cut into triangles. Then for lunch I have a *tarte tropézienne*, thick as a sweet soft loaf, filled with white vanilla-flavoured cream. It's the best moment of a day on which I fail to write anything: the book refuses to be finished. I just can't bring myself to write the closing pages and I think it's quite simply because I don't want to.

I don't want to part from Françoise. I look for her swirling figure as it was that summer. Her new clothes – a woman's clothes – hamper her as much as the child's clothes she wore before. In the one set of clothes she felt restricted, while the other set swamps her, I would say, in imitation of what Bernard Frank says about Benjamin Constant.[60] But, exhilarated and enchanted, she is watching the world watching her.

I see her on the terrace of the La Ponche restaurant. It is the sixties.

The man sharing her table is an Italian who looks like an American film star. He is square-jawed – when he clenches his teeth his cheeks become hollow, in the same great way that the dimple in his chin deepens. He is handsome in a manly way, just as Françoise loves them to be, or, rather, as she will love Bob Westhoff. Together they discuss the cinema of René Clair and Maurice Ronet who is a friend of Françoise's brother; they discuss Alberto Moravia, whom they both know; they discuss the theatre and Laurel and Hardy.

'Yes, I love Italian cinema. *The Easy Life* and of course *La Dolce Vita*, which I saw last year. And most of all Visconti. I love *Rocco and His Brothers*, which I prefer to *The Leopard*,' says Françoise.

'Visconti is a great friend of mine,' replies the enigmatic Italian, without elaborating.

'If there's one of them I find really tedious, though, it's Pasolini,' she goes on. 'I just don't understand his films. Yet I've seen them both, *Mamma Roma* and *Accattone*, but I would be hard put to say which of the two bored me more.'

'It's sometimes good to be a little bored.'

'Oh no, not at the cinema. At least with a book you can close it and put off reading it until later. But at the cinema you're constrained and you're forced to stick it out. There's nothing worse.'

Discussion then moves on merrily to the latest French directors and the famous New Wave. It is getting ever hotter on the terrace of La Ponche. The conversation is most agreeable, but siesta time is approaching, and in high summer that means it's time for love in the afternoon, which no one would miss for anything. Françoise stands up to take her leave.

'It's been lovely having coffee with you,' she says, shading her eyes from the sun.

In response the man raises his white straw hat. 'Likewise. But I haven't introduced myself. I'm Pier Paolo Pasolini. Very pleased to have met you.'

Françoise was not abashed, of that I am sure, nor was Pasolini vexed. They were each too much amused at having been, over coffee, characters in a piece of vaudeville.[61]

Returning to my little rented studio, I quickly write the last scenes of the book, those where we suddenly see the girl, in spite of herself, become the heroine of a novel that she is gearing up to inhabit, declaring to delighted journalists, 'Give me nightclubs, whisky and Ferraris any day, not cooking, knitting or making do'[62] and having to reply to a thousand questions of the type: 'Do you still take the bus?', 'Do you eat noodles?', 'Is the heroine of your novel you?'

In Saint-Tropez, Françoise swops her grey pencil skirts for a blue sailcloth shirt and trousers like those the fishermen wear, she slips her feet into rope sandals from Vachon's, at that time the only shop overlooking the harbour, and she feels free to go clambering over the rocks, as children do. The years for doing the twist in Saint-Tropez have not quite arrived yet, no, we are still in the well-behaved era of beach games, ping-pong matches, reading in the shade of the umbrella pines and drinking cocktails when evening drapes your sun-kissed shoulders in its slightly chilly gauze.

Françoise spends the summer of 1954 in Hossegor with her family, in the holiday house she quit the previous year in order to escape back to Paris and, in the shadow of her father and the shade of the apartment on Boulevard Malesherbes, write the famous book that she told her friends she had 'been writing for a long time', which was a lie. How good it is to turn a lie into truth. Françoise applied herself to the task earnestly and with ardour. Working in Paris in August, while others are away getting their bikinis scorched, is so very pleasant.

Thus a year has passed, and Michel Déon is sent by *Paris Match* to report on the holidays of France's latest idol. It is a summer that will be much less warm than the previous one, that will witness the flight of the first Boeing 707 in its skies, the first playing of 'That's All Right (Mama)' on Radio WHBQ of Memphis, the freeing of the prisoners of Dien Bien Phu and François Truffaut's first short, *Une Visite*, shot in Rue de Douai in the apartment of the editor-in-chief of *Les Cahiers du Cinéma*, with photography by Jacques Rivette and edited by Alain Resnais.

Colette dies on 3 August. Did she, before she died, have time to read the book by the girl whom the newspapers[63] were calling 'an eighteen-year-old Colette'?

On the train home, I read over my almost finished manuscript and I write the following letter to Denis Westhoff:

Dear Denis,
It is several months since we had lunch and you suggested that I should write a book in memory of your mother, or, rather, a book to revive the memory of her. You wanted

to draw attention to a particular period in her life, the one that can be summed up as having 'preceded the legend'. Denis, you presented me with a gift and I have tried to be as true to the task as possible. But in what way true? Most faithful to what? These are questions I have had to answer and I decided to be most faithful to myself, hoping in this way that I would only have to explain myself to one person.

Today, when I reread the manuscript, it seems to me that its 'secret plot' – which is to say, the subject that, although not consciously chosen, emerges when the writing is done – involves an unlikely friendship between a lady of a certain age, now dead, and a young woman born two generations after her. For, from the day we had lunch together, your mother entered my life with all the force of a living being. Initially, I think, your mother did not like me very much. In common with all mothers, she was suspicious of her son's choice of woman; she no doubt found me too glum and too serious. But, as often happens in tales of ill-suited couples thrown together by fate, she has just had to get used to me and I believe I have had the good fortune to become the object of a special affection on her part. Yes, your mother has become for me a confidante, a not very sympathetic one, one who is as amusing as she is severe and as uncompromising as she is joyful. During all those weeks of work, we spoke to each other almost every day and our conversations, which I derived from her books and from her life, were interrupted by nothing and by no one. Like my other friends, she pointed me in the direction of books that I would not otherwise have read, she helped me understand a thousand things that were obscure to me, she propelled me towards people I would perhaps not have considered, she richly filled hours that I would otherwise have let slip by. I do believe that Françoise Sagan has surrounded me with her benevolence, has influenced my actions and thus, in accordance with the butterfly effect, has determined my whole life, the life I have ahead of me – for I believe that to be the role of friends, great friends.

I hope you will not regret having chosen me, for I have given of myself entirely in this book and have written it with the greatest reverence, but also, in honour of your mother, with the greatest degree of irreverence possible.

A.

1 Denis Westhoff, *Sagan et fils*, Stock, 2012.

2 Françoise Sagan, *Réponses*, interviews, éditions Pauvert, 1974.

3 Florence Malraux, in conversation with the author.

4 Alain Vircondelet, *Françoise Sagan, un charmant petit monstre*, Flammarion, 2002.

5 Virginia Woolf, *A Room of One's Own*, The Hogarth Press, 1929. [Translator's note: quoted in French and annotated as 'Virginia Woolf, *Une chambre à soi*, traduction de Clara Malraux, 10/18, 1996'.]

6 Françoise Sagan, *Des bleus à l'âme*, Flammarion, 1972. 'When she was eighteen, she had written a nice little French composition that had been published and had made her famous.' [Translator's note: first published in English as *Scars on the Soul*, translated by Joanna Kilmartin, André Deutsch Limited, 1974.]

7 Françoise Sagan, *Des bleus à l'âme*, op.cit. 'She had refused to make a tragedy out of it all, or even a problem; in any case, writing was, first and foremost, something she enjoyed doing.'

8 Marie-Dominique Lelièvre, *Sagan à toute allure*, Denoël, 2008. 'I like writing,' she said. 'To write a novel is to construct a lie. I like telling lies. I have always lied.'

9 Denis Westhoff, in conversation with the author.

10 Françoise Sagan, *Bonjour tristesse*, Julliard, 1954.

11 Denis Westhoff, *Sagan et fils*, op.cit.

12 Marie-Dominique Lelièvre, *Sagan à toute allure*, op. cit.

13 Ibid.

14 Jean-Claude Lamy, *Françoise Sagan, une légende*, Mercure de France, 2004. 'I said to myself, "Well! It's complicated!" For the first time in my life I had a foreboding that nothing was entirely black or white. In a world torn between Good and Evil, there were grey areas. Things were much more ambiguous than I had imagined.'

15 Sophie Delassein, *Aimez-vous Sagan...*, Fayard, 2002. 'Françoise Sagan often tells how, at that time – whether it be an exact memory or one that has been embellished – she went to consult a fortune-teller based in Rue de l'Abbé -Groult, who is supposed to have predicted, "You will write a book that will cross the oceans." '

16 Christer Strömholm, *Le Boulevard*, introduction to the book of photographs *Les Amies de Place Blanche*, VU éditions, 2011.

17 Interview with Françoise Sagan on France Culture in 1955, quoted by Thierry Séchan, *Le Roman de Sagan*, Romart, 2013. 'I don't know why it is so difficult to speak of luck. I myself am quite well acquainted with luck. Luck came my way a year ago and has been with me ever since.'

18 Preface by Claude Mauriac to the album *Mauriac intime*, photographs by Jeanne François-Mauriac, Stock, 1985.

19 Jean-Claude Lamy, *Françoise Sagan, une légende*, op.cit.

20 Jean-Claude Lamy, *René Julliard*, Julliard, 1992.

21 Bertrand Meyer-Stabley, *Les Dames de l'Élysée. Celles d'hier et de demain*, Librairie académique Perrin, 1999.

22 Henry de Montherlant, *Les Jeunes Filles*, Grasset, 1947.

23 Vladimir Jankélévitch, *L'Imprescriptible*, Seuil, 1986.

24 Marie-Dominique Lelièvre, *Sagan à toute allure*, op. cit.

25 Denis Westhoff, in conversation with the author.

26 Denis Westhoff, *Sagan et fils*, op. cit.

27 Françoise Sagan, *Avec mon meilleur souvenir*, Gallimard, 1984.

28 Boni de Castellane, *Mémoires*, introduction by Emmanuel de Waresquiel, Perrin, 1986.

29 Marcel Proust, *Le Côté de Guermantes*, Gallimard, 1921–1922.

30 Françoise Sagan, *Bonjour Tristesse*, op. cit.

31 Jean-Claude Lamy, *Françoise Sagan, une légende*, op. cit.

32 Interview with Françoise Sagan for *La Dépêche*, quoted by Jean-Claude Lamy, *Françoise Sagan, une légende*, op. cit. 'Cajarc and my childhood: an enchanting domain that must for ever remain inviolate.'

33 Françoise Sagan, *De guerre lasse*, Gallimard, 1986.

34 Jean-Claude Lamy, *Françoise Sagan, une légende*, op. cit.

35 The person in question was the actor Michel Simon, according to Michel Castaing in his article in the newspaper *Le Monde*, dated 1 February 1994.

36 Marie-Dominique Lelièvre, *Sagan à toute allure*, op. cit. 'What impression did the death of that child from dehydration leave on his family? Was he the victim of the adults' inadvertence? The question meets with a blank: Suzanne Quoirez does not really remember. As for Sagan's biographers, they draw a veil over the event.'

37 Alain Vircondelet, *Françoise Sagan, un charmant petit monstre*, op. cit.

38 David Teboul, *Bardot, la méprise*, Gaumont Télévision, Christian Davin production, Arte France, 2011.

39 Françoise Sagan, *Derrière épaule...*, Plon, 1998. 'It was a summer just like the summers we still used to have back then, broken up by dusty, deserted avenues beneath trees of apple green and dark green ... I go to the baker's in Rue Jouffroy in my dressing gown and buy two croissants. I nibble mine on

the way back, meeting only a bus as empty as the boulevard and an ill-shaven bachelor.'

40 Marie-Dominique Lelièvre, *Sagan à toute allure*, op. cit.

41 In the original anecdote, the person who arrived was a journalist. Recounted by Denis Westhoff, *Sagan et fils*, op.cit.

42 Denis Westhoff, *Sagan et fils*, op. cit.

43 Sophie Delassein, *Aimez-vous Sagan…*, op. cit.

44 Marie-Dominique Lelièvre, *Sagan à toute allure*, op. cit.

45 Marguerite Duras, *Les Petits Chevaux de Tarquinia*, Gallimard, 1953.

46 Matthieu Galey, *Journal 1953–1973*, Grasset, 1987.

47 Alain Malraux, *Les Marronniers de Boulogne: Malraux père introuvable*, Bartillat, 2012.

48 Frédérique Lebelley, *Duras ou le poids d'une plume*, Grasset, 1994.

49 Marguerite Duras, *La Cuisine de Marguerite*, Benoît Jacob, 1999. Quoted by Laetitia Cénac, *Marguerite Duras. L'écriture de la passion*, La Martinière, 2013.

50 Jean-Claude Lamy, *Françoise Sagan, une légende*, op. cit.

51 Thierry Séchan, *Le Roman de Sagan*, op. cit.

52 Marie-Dominique Lelièvre, *Sagan à toute allure*, op. cit.

53 Alain Vircondelet, *Françoise Sagan, un charmant petit monstre*, op. cit.

54 Thierry Séchan, *Le Roman de Sagan*, op. cit.

55 Denis Westhoff, *Sagan et fils*, op. cit.

56 Françoise Sagan, *Avec mon meilleur souvenir*, op. cit.

57 Tennessee Williams, 'On Meeting a Young Writer', *Harper's Bazaar*, August 1956, reprinted in Tennessee Williams, *New Selected Essays: Where I Live*, New Directions Paperbook, ed. John S. Bak, foreword by John Lahr, 2009. [Translator's note: quoted in French and annotated as 'Tennessee Williams,

De vous à moi, éditions Baker Street, translated by Martine Leroy-Battistelli, 2011'.]

58 Françoise Sagan, *Avec mon meilleur souvenir*, op. cit.

59 Jean Cocteau, *Le Passé défini*, journal, Gallimard, 2005.

60 Marie-Dominique Lelièvre, *Sagan à toute allure*, op. cit.

61 Denis Westhoff, *Sagan et fils*, op. cit.

62 Ibid.

63 Michel Déon, in an article for *Paris Match*: '*Bonjour Tristesse* introduces us to an eighteen-year-old writer ... A novelist of high calibre is born, perhaps a new Colette, to judge by the precocious qualities of the work. Critics will be on the lookout for Françoise's second novel.'

BIBLIOGRAPHY

Laure Adler and Stefan Bollmann, *Les femmes qui écrivent vivent dangereusement*, Flammarion, 2007.

Marie-Thérèse Bartoli, *Chère Madame Sagan*, Jean-Jacques Pauvert, 2002.

Laetitia Cénac, *Marguerite Duras. L'écriture de la passion*, La Martinière, 2013.

Jean Cocteau, *Le Passé défini*, vols III and IV, Gallimard, 2005.

Anne Crestani and Claude Dubois, *Paris années 1950*, Geste Éditions, 2011.

Sophie Delassein, *Aimez-vous Sagan...*, Fayard, 2002.

Michel Déon, *Bagages pour Vancouver*, stories, La Table Ronde, 1985.

Georges Didi-Huberman, *L'Album de l'art à l'époque du* Musée imaginaire, Hazan, 2013.

Guillaume Durand, *Il était une fois Sagan*, Jacques-Marie Laffont, 2005.

Annie Ernaux, *Les Années*, Gallimard, 2008.

Bernard Frank, *5, rue des Italiens*, Grasset, 2007.

Bernard Frank, *Mon siècle*, Julliard, 1993.

Matthieu Galey, *Journal*, Grasset, 1987, 1989.

Jérôme Garcin, *Littérature vagabonde*, Flammarion, 2009.

Annick Geille, *Un amour de Sagan*, Pauvert, 2007.

Juan Goytisolo, *Genet à Barcelone*, Fayard, 2012.

Julia Kristeva, *Le Génie féminin 3, Colette*, Fayard, 2002.

Jean-Claude Lamy, *Françoise Sagan, une légende*, Mercure de France, 2004.

Jean-Claude Lamy, *René Julliard*, Julliard, 1992.

Marie-Dominique Lelièvre, *Sagan à toute allure*, Denoël, 2008.

Pascal Louvrier, *Sagan, un chagrin immobile*, Hugo et Compagnie, 2012.

Alain Malraux, *Les marronniers de Boulogne: Malraux père introuvable*, Bartillat, 2012.

Clara Malraux, *Et pourtant j'étais libre*, Grasset, 1979.

Gohier-Marvier, *Bonjour Françoise!*, Grand Damier, 1957.

François Mauriac, *Bloc-Notes*, Seuil, 1993.

Geneviève Moll, *Madame Sagan*, Ramsay, 2005.

Bertrand Poirot-Delpech, *Bonjour Sagan*, Herscher, 1985.

Élisabeth Quin, *Bel de nuit, Gerald Nanty*, Grasset, 2007.

Bertrand Poirot-Delpech, *Bonjour Sagan*, Herscher, 1985.

.